DETERMINED PRINCE

CAPTURED BY A DRAGON-SHIFTER: A QURILIXEN
WORLD SHORT NOVEL

MICHELLE M. PILLOW

MICHELLE M. PILLOW® - MICHELLEPILLOW.COM

Determined Prince © Copyright 2014 - 2018 by Michelle M. Pillow

Second Printing July 2018

First Printing November 2014

First Electronic Printing December 2014, The Raven Books

Cover art © Copyright 2014

ISBN-13: 978-1-62501-181-7

Published by The Raven Books LLC

ABOUT DETERMINED PRINCE

Welcome to the dangerous world of Qurilixen where dragon-shifters and cat-shifters rule as fiercely as they love.

DRAGON SHIFTER PRINCE Kyran and his people are gravely in need of mates. Their planet's female shifters are dying out, so they look to Earth for new women. Vivacious Eve catches Kyran's eye — but claiming her will be harder than he anticipated...

Dragon-shifter Prince Kyran has studied the Earth people and is ready to assimilate. Female shifters are all but going extinct on his planet of Qurilixen, and his people are desperate for mates—so much so they're taking matters into their own hands. What better place to capture a woman than Earth? After all, dragon-shifters had come from there centuries ago. Surely a human female would be honored to be selected by one as fine and fierce as himself?

While on Earth, Kyran stumbles upon the most beautiful woman he's ever imagined, singing something the natives call rock 'n' roll. His blood simmers and he knows Eve is the one for him. But taming this feisty female is going to take much more than his training prepared him for.

WELCOME TO QURILIXEN

Qurilixen World Novels

Dragon Lords Series

Barbarian Prince

Perfect Prince

Dark Prince

Warrior Prince

His Highness The Duke

The Stubborn Lord

The Reluctant Lord

The Impatient Lord

The Dragon's Queen

Lords of the Var® Series
The Savage King

The Playful Prince

The Bound Prince

The Rogue Prince

The Pirate Prince

Captured by a Dragon-Shifter Series
Determined Prince

Rebellious Prince

Stranded with the Cajun

Hunted by the Dragon

Mischievous Prince

Headstrong Prince

Space Lords Series
His Frost Maiden

His Fire Maiden

His Metal Maiden

His Earth Maiden

His Woodland Maiden

Dynasty Lords Series

Seduction of the Phoenix

Temptation of the Butterfly

To learn more about the Qurilixen World series of books and to stay up to date on the latest book list visit www.MichellePillow.com

AUTHOR UPDATES

To stay informed about when a new book in the
series installments is released, sign up for updates:

michellepillow.com/author-updates

NOTE FROM AUTHOR

IF YOU'RE new to my books, the *Dragon Lords* are my bestselling futuristic shape-shifter romance series. The stories became reader favorites, and so I wrote things from their enemy's point of view in a spin-off series for the cat-shifting *Lords of the Var*®. Then they ventured off into the stars in the series installment *Space Lords*. Now, I'm time traveling with them back to our time with the series *Captured by a Dragon-Shifter*, which you are now reading book one of. Don't worry, I have the series reading order on my website to help you figure it all out, http://michellepillow.com/.

To those of you not new to my books, readers have emailed asking Dragon Lords cultural questions since the first dragon-shifting prince released years ago. I have teased you with a lot of little hints of how the Draig found brides in "the old days". Many of you have expressed wanting to climb aboard the space ship and sail away into the future—which would probably take some cryogenic freezing and a lot of icy waiting. Well, before you start packing those sweaters... I don't want any of you going to that extreme, so I've brought your favorite dragon-shifters and cat-shifters to modern-day Earth. They don't live on our planet, but they have recently started to revisit.

For *Dragon Lords* and *Lords of the Var*® fans, *Captured by a Dragon-Shifter* is a modern-day prequel series to those first books. They take place long before the princes you know and love ever found their mates, long before *The Dragon's Queen*, in a time when the dragon-shifters and cat-shifters actually—wait for it—*liked* each other and hung out as friends. They also don't have Galaxy Brides to bring them women. There's no one left to marry on the planet and things are starting to get desperate.

AUTHOR RECOMMENDS READING series installments in order of release for the simple fact she likes hiding little tidbits in the books as she goes and it's more fun that way, though each book can be read as a standalone if you prefer.

To the dreamers and star gazers

CHAPTER ONE

DRAIG NORTHERN MOUNTAINS, PLANET
OF QURILIXEN, THE NEAR FUTURE

PRINCE KYRAN ADJUSTED the bandana around his neck as he peered deeper into the dark cave hidden within the mountain. At least, he was fairly sure the thing around his neck was called a bandana. Or was it a handkerchief? It was hard to remember all the human words. Technically, his people still spoke a dialect of an Earth language, but so much had changed in the centuries since they'd left the planet, that many new words and customs had to be learned.

"My name is Kyran. You look like an honorable woman," he whispered, practicing what he would say to any prospective mate. "I have a home with my parents and my brother. There we will live and you will be part of our family. Would you like to give me many children?"

Behind him, the mountain valley air was sweet, a blend of grasses and tiny blue flowers. It mixed with the almost acidic smell of porous black rocks now surrounding him. It wasn't the darkness that caused the tiny jolt of apprehension in his stomach. His shifter eyes could easily cut through the shadows. It was what awaited him beyond the dark stone walls —marriage.

Kyran smiled thoughtfully to himself, perhaps simple was best. "Come to my home planet and I will make you my princess."

The Draig, Kyran's people, were a race of dragon-shifters. Long ago, they'd escaped Earth, using a portal to come to a place where they could live out in the open, free of persecution. The Var, friends of the Draig people, had come with them. Vars were cat-shifters and had just as much reason to leave the old world. Only by working together had the two races managed to make a clean start. It was an alliance so strong that Kyran couldn't imagine it ever changing.

Perhaps he should try poetic. "You will like my planet. Qurilixen is a wondrous place bathed in almost constant daylight. In the valley near the borderlands, there is a forest of oversized trees—so big that from a distance the taller ones look like your castle homes on Earth. Here we will join and become one."

Though he'd never actually been to Earth himself, Kyran had seen pictures of the old palaces in the royal library, and they were very much like the castle he and his family lived in. Only some of the elders could actually remember making the trip across, and they had been little help as to what to expect. A few scouts had been through the portal to study modern Earth and to make sure the trip would be safe. They spoke of tall square castles and loud noises.

"This will be easy," he told himself in determination. "Earth has many women. Finding one will not be hard. I have studied the transmissions. I am ready for this assimilation into Earth culture. I am a fierce dragon and will make a fine husband. A woman would be lucky to have me. I will find a princess." Fear tried to work its way into his brain, but he pushed it aside. He had to stay determined. This had to work—not only for him, but for his people.

Luckily, Earth had advanced to a state that humans aired transmissions. They called it television, and once the shifters had learned to capture those waves, they'd been able to study the new Earth culture to practice blending in.

"How-ow-dee-ee," he sounded out slowly, trying to mimic the wavy intonation of the customary greeting. He liked the cowmen. They appeared to be a tough breed of humans who spent much time outdoors riding funny looking ceffyls around open fields.

Blending was better than the royals' original plan of sneaking through the portal and kidnapping human women like the barbaric tribes written about in old scrolls. At least this way, they could get a good look at the females before they snatched them. To some, the idea seemed extreme—bringing women through the portal in order to marry them. It had taken decades before enough of the elders had finally agreed to the plan. Unfortunately, the Draig and Var no longer had a choice. If they didn't find compatible mates soon, their kind would die out in a generation. The few alien species who had made contact were not mating material for a number of reasons—incompatible biology, conflicting customs, no desire to live onworld.

For some reason, female shifters were no longer being born. The males thrived, growing stronger, living much longer than before. Couples had even been encouraged to have more babies to up the odds. Nothing worked. Now they had a large generation of men with little hope of marriage. Their best scholars were working on the problem, but until a solution was found, for the sake of their survival, they needed to find brides.

Historical documents indicated humans were reproductively compatible. This portal was their best hope, a way for the men of their planet to have a chance at happiness.

Their ancestors had caved in the portal when they'd first arrived on Qurilixen. Apparently, they'd thought no one would ever want to go back and wished to keep humans from following. Only after years of digging had the Draig unearthed it. Prince Kyran would be one of the first four grooms to go through. It was his duty to show the people this plan would work.

Many elders weren't happy with the plan to find mates this way, for they still carried the emotional scars from the old days. Human religions had changed, and with their new beliefs had come the idea that all shifters had made pacts with some person named Demon. If there were signed treaties with this Demon, any records had been lost.

Some shifters hoped time had changed the

humans. Because of the controversy, the four princes had volunteered to go first and prove this could work. Prince Kyran and his younger brother, Prince Finn of the Draig, would join Princes Ivar and Rafe of the Var. It wasn't decreed which of them would come back with a bride, only that they had to start looking.

"Ready?" Finn asked, coming from behind Kyran carrying a torch. He glanced over Kyran's outfit and smirked.

"What?" Kyran looked down. He looked exactly like a cowman with boots, a hat and tight pants. Actually, he'd chosen the style of dress for the tight pants. What better way to show off one of his finer assets? "It's better than what you picked."

Finn grinned. He was dressed as a great warrior. "We shall see who turns the most heads, brother."

Hearing a noise, both dragon-shifters turned. Prince Ivar's green gaze glinted from the darkened shadows. When he stepped forward into the torch-light, he wore the native clothing of the cat-shifters. Fitted black pants pulled low across the hips, showing off a fair amount of stomach. The matching black shirt was laced down the center front, revealing a strip of his chest. Kyran quirked a brow.

Ivar waved a hand in dismissal. "The tailor brought me a gown and said I was to go to this accursed planet in it. I refused. I much rather receive stares than blend in as a woman—royal Earth custom or not. What is a *draqueen* anyway? It sounds like your ancestors, not mine, dragons."

Kyran shared a look with his brother. Finn shrugged. He didn't know either.

"Where's Rafe?" Kyran asked. "The portal's about to open."

"Here!" Prince Rafe called. His footfall sounded over the cave as he jogged forward. His white pants belled wide at the bottom, matching the white long-sleeved shirt. Rafe glanced at his brother's non-attire and said distractedly, "Sorry."

The more serious Ivar grunted. "You lost track of time before *this*?"

"I felt like someone was following me. I doubled back to the borderlands before returning," Rafe said. Then defensively, he added to Ivar, "You think I'm paranoid, but I'm telling you, not every Var wants to see us marry humans. Arguments are still being made that taking humans will dilute shifter blood and cause us to lose our natural abilities. They would rather we take to the stars and meet other humanoid species or wait for the gods to bless us."

"It is not their place to question a Var royal

decree," Ivar stated to his brother. "The elder council had their say. This will be."

"Shall we?" Kyran wanted to stop the two cat-shifter brothers before they began yelling. Moving to walk deeper into the cave, he glanced over his shoulder to see if the others followed.

"I don't know why you're so eager to meet your destiny, Kyran," Finn said.

"Aren't you?" Rafe asked. "I can't wait to find a bride to share my bed. The women ships don't come often enough for my taste."

"I've told you to stay away from those ships. You do not know what diseases the alien travelers carry in their profession," Ivar said.

"I only watch them dance," Rafe defended. He let fur sprout over his nose as he made a face at his brother's back. Finn hid his laugh.

"What if you get a shrew?" Ivar sounded reasonable, like always.

"So long as she's shrewing in my bed, I don't care." Rafe winked.

Ivar grunted by way of an answer.

Kyran knew Rafe loved nothing more than to aggravate his stoic brother. "Come. The time is soon. Remember, only one is to find a bride this time. They want us to take it slowly."

"And I elect Kyran." Finn laughed, slapping his older brother's shoulder so hard Kyran stumbled. "This was his idea."

"Agreed," Rafe said quickly, not breaking stride.

Kyran opened his mouth as he righted himself, but Ivar had said, "Agreed," before he could get a word in. The three princes laughed. Kyran took a deep breath. He knew his duty, and if he must go first to ensure the future of his people, so be it.

"Ach! Come on then. Now is as good as later." Kyran forced a chuckle, not wanting to admit he was nervous. "So help me, when I'm finished you all had better go next. I'll not be the only prince settled."

CHAPTER TWO

CLEVELAND, OHIO, EARTH

SMOKE FILLED THE CLUB, but Eve Minott ignored it from her place on stage. Slinging her guitar over her back, she grabbed the microphone, closed her eyes to the bright spotlight and sang her heart out. The beat was heavy, pounding, vicious—and she loved it. No whiny, poppy, girly music for her. She played hardcore in-your-face rock.

The club was one of many in a section of the city known as The Flats. The strip of underground bars and restaurants ran along the banks of the Cuyahoga River. At night, lights lit up the area and gleamed off the water, back-dropped by the industrial arches of a bridge.

Cleveland was just another stop on the map for Eve. She wasn't famous, but she didn't care. She adored music and was happy doing what she loved. Besides, living the night life meant she didn't have to get up early in the morning for a boring day job.

The song ended abruptly. The crowd cheered. A man whistled. Eve threw her hands up into the air and grinned, loving the attention. Instantly, the drum beat sounded again, kicking off the next song. She banged her head to the fast tempo as she whipped her guitar around and began playing along. The lights dimmed, not as blinding as before and colors swirled over the sea of heads before her. The smoke cleared and she was glad for it. She was able to make out more of the crowd now.

Her skimpy tank top clung to her sweaty flesh and her tight vinyl pants were hot as hell. Even with the doors open, the hot breeze did little to cool the stage. She felt strands of her long hair tickling her back even though it was pulled up messily on top of her head.

Endless faces moved, bouncing before her as the crowd jumped to the beat, their hands tossed up in tribute of the old classic Eve had reworked. She turned, grinning at her band mates—all women except for Paul on the drums. They teasingly called him their sex kitten. Paul winked, his drumsticks flying through the air like a baton for a moment before he caught them. Eve laughed before turning back to her mic.

Belting out the words, she watched the crowd part before her. The movement caught her eye and it was all she could do not to laugh over her words. Four very large, very odd men stood motionless surrounded by swaying bodies close to the stage.

The first, dressed as a sailor from the fifties in white bell-bottoms and a matching shirt, was grinning like a fool as he watched some nearby women dance—or more accurately, as he watched their breasts jiggle as they danced. He stood next to a black-clad ninja with dark brown hair and sinfully dark eyes. It was impossible to see most of the ninja's face under the mask.

Next to the ninja was the biggest of the men in a vest minus an undershirt. The expanses of his bulging muscles were easy enough to see from the stage. His tight, hip-hugger pants dipped so low she saw his flat stomach and hip bones in the flashing light. Naughty biker, perhaps?

Last in line was a cowboy. Eve's voice dipped, ending too fast on a note. She quickly recovered, screaming into the mic. The cowboy flinched at the sound even as the crowd went wild. She guessed he was more of a country fan. Eve again tried not to laugh as she tore her eyes away for a brief moment before looking back.

The sexy cowboy was staring at her intently, his arms folded over his chest, his body unmoving. His bright eyes shone in the dimmed lights, as if they held an inner glow. They were light in color—blue, perhaps green. Rich black hair flowed to his shoulders from beneath his white hat. Long sideburns trailed down his jaw, framing his full, kissable lips. Eve felt a twinge of desire in her stomach, making her nerves all that more alive. She ignored it, tearing her eyes from him.

In truth, all four men were hot male specimens—even if they wore flamboyant costumes in the middle of summer. They only spoke to each other, though women did try to get their attention. However, sailor boy's head was bobbing along with the dancing breasts.

The song ended, the notes trailing off amongst the cheers. Eve bowed, holding on to her guitar. She flashed an impish smile at the crowd. Sweat made her skin glisten and she was out of breath, but she didn't care.

A slower melody started signaling their last song of the night. She might not be the king of rock and roll, but she sure as hell was going to sing like she was the queen. The cowboy lowered his arms slowly to his side and tilted his head to stare at her. She found herself staring back, unable to look away, singing directly to him. Emotion always filled her when she sang, and she felt it pour out of her into the mystery man. It was only the cheering of the crowd that made her realize the song was over. She took several deep breaths, smiling as she tore her eyes away from the cowboy.

It had been a stellar performance and she'd sung like it was her last show on Earth. After a few moments, she yelled goodnight and sauntered off the stage. A small room in the back was reserved for the band. Eve dropped off her guitar, knowing she'd probably crash on the old couch for the night. It's not like she had an apartment to go back to. It was either the old couch or camping in Paul's van.

"Good set, baby," Paul said, coming in after her. He tossed his drumsticks next to her case. He'd long since thrown off his T-shirt and stood next to her in a pair of old denim jeans. They were so faded and worn that the legs had holes in them that he'd safety pinned back together.

"Shit, it's hot tonight," said the bassist, Kim. She wore a tight skirt and a blood-red corset. "I need a drink."

"Mm," Eve laughed. "Me too."

"Me three," Joan, who also played guitar, agreed. She scratched her short red hair, causing it to spike. Kim slung her arm over Joan's shoulder and kissed her cheek. They shared a loving look.

"Me four," Eve said. "And five."

"Come on, baby, let's get a drink." Paul grabbed Eve and slung her over his shoulder, her slender frame no match for his bigger strength. Kicking her feet, she squealed with laughter as he carted her into the crowd. Cheers sounded as people saw them.

Paul slapped her ass playfully before setting her down next to the wooden bar. Eve grinned as he yelled at the bartender for a couple of beers and shots of tequila. Since the beginning—which truth be told, was only three months ago—there had never been anything between them, only friendship born of a shared wanderlust. "I think it's time for a birthday toast, don't you, sweetheart?"

"Damn straight, pussycat," Eve yelled, raising her voice over the noisy juke box that had taken over their job of inciting the crowd. "Let's show these savages what rock 'n roll is all about!"

CHAPTER THREE

KYRAN GLANCED around the noisy club. The humans seemed happy to be there, even though the music was loud and angry. Still, there was something very raw and primitive to the beat of it—not to mention the very sexy woman who'd been singing. Though during the last song, the slow one, he'd found he enjoyed the strange melody and softer caress of her voice.

Too bad the singer looked like a bundle of trouble. When she'd belted her first songs with such pent-up anger and aggression, he'd known he'd be better off finding another to take home with him. Moreover, her dark brown hair was growing blue in places. There was no telling how humans had evolved. It was quite possible the blue was a mutational defect. It wasn't exactly a look suited to a future queen of the Draig—or his heirs for that matter. What if his sons had blue patches on their heads when they shifted?

"Have you decided?" Finn asked, eyeing a group of females.

"Point her out so we can grab her and leave." Ivar shifted his weight as he looked dispassionately around. "This world is more savage than I feared. I'm not sure it makes much difference if you pick one woman over another."

"What? We get off Qurilixen and you don't want to have some fun? Who's to know if we test the fighting skills of some of these men? Or if we sample the finer wares? Many of these women appear willing." Rafe laughed. "I say take your time, Kyran. There's no reason to rush this. Mating is forever, you know."

"The gods will show me," Kyran said, certain of that fact. "I'll feel it."

"It would be nice if there was something to help you decide," Finn mused. "Like a rod that heated up when pointed at your mate. Then you could aim it around, find a suitable match and be done with it. I don't like this random, glance around, pick a pretty *fea*, grab her and hope for the best for the rest of your life. Perhaps we should take several of them and then decide later."

"Ah, now *that's* an idea." Rafe nodded enthusiastically. "Can we please?"

Kyran's stomach knotted. He'd been thinking pretty much the same thing. Though instead of agreeing, he said, "You must trust in the gods to lead you down the right path. That is why we spent last week at the temple."

"Mm, I thought that was because of the priestesses." Rafe grinned, giving a nearby group of ladies an audacious wink.

"Can't you at least take the gods seriously?" Ivar frowned.

"Why?" Rafe mumbled, his eyes caught by a woman in a short skirt as she walked by. She turned her head and her gaze lingered on Ivar. The man didn't notice. Rafe sighed, shaking his head. "You take things seriously enough for everyone."

"What are you guys supposed to be?" A woman with short black hair stopped in front of them, her arms linked with two blonde friends. She had to yell over the music to be heard. The blondes' giggles were lost in the noise.

"I am Kyran," he said, bowing his head. His voice was gruffer in speech than the humans' accents, but there was nothing to be done for it.

"Oh, you're European!" one of the blondes exclaimed, batting her eyelashes at Ivar.

"No, I am a *draqueen*," Ivar stated bluntly.

"Drag queens, eh? I should've known," the black-haired woman answered. She frowned as the three of them looked the princes over. "Well now, that's a real pity, boys. You come find us if you decide to swing both ways."

The four princes watched the women dance off into the crowd.

"Perhaps, we should tell them we're European," Rafe mused. "That is at least the tenth time you scared females off by saying you're a *draqueen*. Maybe they're not used to talking to royalty."

"Good idea," Kyran said.

"Perhaps we should have brought the scouts with us," Ivar stated.

"So they could report back to our parents?" Rafe snorted. "I think not."

"Let's go procure drinks. Do we have that trading paper?" Kyran asked before the brothers could start arguing.

"The transmissions say it is called cabbage or dinero or cash money," Rafe explained, reaching into his white pants. "Ah, yeah, I... Here it is."

Kyran swiped it from him and walked toward the bar. He placed his palm flat on the wooden top. A man came up from behind. "What'll it be?"

"Four firewaters—" Kyran paused, trying to remember the words they'd been told to use, "—ah...amigo."

"Sorry, buddy, don't know how to make a fire-water amigo," the man answered.

Kyran glanced around. Seeing a tall glass of pink liquid in front of the woman next to him, he pointed and said, "Give me that."

"Twenty," the man said, leaving to pour the drinks. Kyran glanced around and then shrugged. Twenty what?

As he waited, he again scanned the crowd. There were several pretty ladies, but none he wanted to take home to be his bride. Many were too loud, too gaudily dressed, hanging too freely on other men—some of them two or more. One thing was for sure, when he got his bride home, he would not be allowing her to touch other men like this. Such things were not done. Maybe it was time they tried another location. Surely they couldn't be faulted for not getting it right the first time.

The man came back with the four drinks. Kyran put the colorful trading paper down on the counter. "Many thanks."

"Twenty," the man repeated.

"Ah," Kyran nodded in understanding as he gestured down to the papers.

The man picked it up. "Sorry, buddy, does this look like a bank? I need twenty American."

"We're European," Finn said.

"That's nice, fellas, but we only accept American money here."

Kyran took a deep breath. He was about to refuse the drinks when a husky feminine voice stopped him. "Just put this round on my tab, Bill."

He saw Finn smile. Kyran turned. It was the blue-brown-haired singer.

"And get me another shot of to-kill-ya, would ya?" she added.

"One tequila comin' up," Bill answered. He didn't move far as he poured a drink into a tiny glass. Kyran assumed she didn't drink too much, being as she was so small compared to a man of his size.

The singer winked at him and he found himself

staring into her hazel green eyes in surprise. "Howdy, partner. Is that a pistol in your pocket?"

Kyran glanced down, patting his waist. He didn't have anything. The woman laughed. It was a nice sound, deep and honest.

She pinched the tiny glass and then tossed her head back to drink. Gasping afterward, she slid the glass toward Bill. "Give me another."

"Anything for you, love." Bill blew her a kiss.

Kyran stiffened, balling his hands into fists, ready to fight the man for the woman's attention. Ivar placed a hand on his arm and shook his head once. Kyran forced himself to relax. Nodding, he picked up the drink she'd gotten for him and said, "Many thanks, m'lady."

The woman gave him a big smile and then turned her attention to the others. Kyran didn't drink but set the glass back down as he studied her. She had an impish grin that went well with her sparkling dark-lined eyes. If he'd been asked what he was looking for in a mate, she wouldn't have been his description. Still, there was something inside him—a primal, urgent lust that called out to her. His body tightened, becoming aroused. He was thankful for his tight jeans, as it kept the blood from flowing too readily into his shaft.

The singer took another drink, tilting her head back in the same quick fashion as before. She motioned to the bartender for another. The man was there with the bottle, instantly pouring one. She drank that one as well, gasping for breath afterward. "Whew, that's what I'm talking about!"

Kyran wondered if maybe it'd be smarter for her to buy a larger glass. Then she wouldn't have to keep refilling it when she was thirsty. Bill refilled the dainty glass yet again and then left to help other customers. Kyran was glad the man was gone. The woman studied the other princes intently.

"I get ninja boy here and the Navy scene, but—" the woman pointed at Ivar, "—what are you supposed to be?"

"Prince Ivar of the Var." Ivar bowed his head.

"We're European," Finn offered quickly.

"Really." The woman chuckled, only to wryly add, "I would've taken you boys for locals."

Kyran tensed as her gaze again met his. For some reason, he couldn't force himself speak. He didn't know what to say to her.

"Dance with me, cowboy," the woman said, her tone dipping slightly. His body lurched with excitement. She leaned close and licked her lips. "It's my birthday and I want to celebrate."

"You look like an honorable planet. I have a home and a brother," he said, nervously trying to get out his preplanned speech. "The trees are castles."

"English isn't your first language, is it? No worries, I don't need you for conversation." Stealing the hat from his head, she sauntered onto the dance floor, joining the crowd. Her slender body swayed to the music as she wound her arms above her head. Kyran tilted his head to the side as he watched her hips. He didn't follow her, only stared.

"Well?" Rafe broke into his daze, thrusting one of the pink drinks at him. "This one seems to like you. Why don't you go see if you like her?"

"I didn't detect a man's mark on her or a finger shackle," Ivar said. "She doesn't appear to be taken or owned."

"She's pretty, though strange." Finn patted his brother's shoulder. "I'm confident the hair can be fixed. It could be worse. I saw a woman whose locks were pink."

"She did not run when I told her who I was," Ivar added logically. "It should make for an easy adjustment to our planet."

The men nodded thoughtfully, each taking a drink of the pink liquor at the same time. Kyran gagged and they each spit the disgusting drink out. A few nearby females screeched in protest as it sprayed by their feet. The women stormed off. The princes quickly set the glasses down.

"Vile," Rafe exclaimed. "How can humans drink that?"

"I'm not sure..." Kyran began, still unnerved from having the woman stand so close. Her lips had been right within reach and he'd wanted nothing more than to kiss her. Just then, the man who'd been on stage making music with the singer danced to where she was on the floor. As the man swept her off the ground, tossed her over his shoulder and danced her about in circles, she held onto Kyran's hat.

Kyran's gut tightened in annoyance. The woman screamed, her laugh ringing over the crowd. Who was this man? Why did she let him grab her?

"You missed your chance," Ivar stated. "That other male is about to claim her for himself."

"You think that's what he is doing?" Finn wondered aloud. "It would make sense. Didn't some of the elders say human men would ride into the village and cart the woman of his choice off? What did they call them?"

"Raiders," Rafe answered. "Or Vikings."

"Perhaps this will be easier than we feared. If women are used to being claimed in such a method, they will offer little protest us stealing them away to our home." Ivar sighed. "Look, he's putting her down. He must have changed his mind. Go, quick, and claim that one so we can get back to the portal. There's really no guarantee how long it will be open. The portal is old. What if it stops working?"

"Do we have to?" Rafe pouted. "But—"

"You will find your mate soon enough, brother. Patience," Ivar said.

"Who's talking about a mate?" Rafe grumbled. "I'm talking about carnal *mating*."

Kyran didn't bother to interrupt as he strode onto the dance floor. It was decided. He would claim her and be done with it. Besides, there was something about her that stirred his blood. She would make a fine bed partner. Someone with so much energy would be lively between the sheets. A woman would have to be spirited to satisfy her Draig husband's sensual needs.

As for the hair, if it could not be fixed, he would order her to cover it with a headdress. Many of the alien species they'd come across had such anomalies if not more. Surely he was just being paranoid about the other Draigs accepting her. If she acted like a queen, as he would instruct her to do, there would be no problem.

He let a slow grin spread over his features. The idea of bedding her brought him much pleasure. No more nights alone stroking himself to completion. Kyran relished the idea of a willing woman, but even more so of a wife.

His body hard with arousal, he stepped up to her, standing still as her eyes met his. Her smile faded some and she stopped dancing. The crowd swayed around them, but Kyran didn't care. All he saw was her.

"I choose you, m'lady," he stated.

She pursed her lips and rocked lightly on her feet. Her words a little slurred, she asked, "Do ya now, cowboy?"

"I am a cowman."

"Are you?"

"Yes, I am not a boy. I earned my manhood many years ago in battle. I choose you."

"Is that so, cow *man*?"

"Yes." The statement was simple, truthful. He had chosen her. This woman was now his bride. His stomach clenched as he waited for her reaction. It wasn't what he'd expected.

The woman lifted up on her toes and pressed her mouth boldly to his. The contact took him by surprise and he didn't react quickly enough. A low hum sounded and then she pulled away, dancing once more.

"Don't you guys usually say ma'am, not m'lady? I think you're getting your cowman confused with a knight in shining armor." The woman winked at him and tipped down his hat so it shaded her eyes. It didn't matter. He saw through the darker shadows over her face. "So which are you? Cowman or knight?"

"Tonight? Both."

"Hmm, and what makes you think I would choose you?"

He nodded in approval. It was a wise question. He should have to prove himself somewhat. Instead of using his voice, he spoke to her as she had him. He reached for her and then lifted her before him and placed his lips firmly to hers. She gasped but didn't fight to be let down as he opened his mouth. The sting of liquor met his tongue, and a second later, she had her legs wrapped around him and was kissing him deeply as if she would devour him.

He held her easily. Humans were so frail compared to the heavier weight of dragon-shifter women. A little moan escaped her when he devoured her in return. Finally, pushing away, she breathed heavily and whispered, "Well, happy birthday to me."

He grinned and set her down on the floor once more. She smiled, her eyes flirty and light. There was interest in her gaze. He knew when a woman's face revealed her attraction for him and hers showed it tenfold. Plus, he detected her desire for him, tasted it on his lips. It was sweet, tempting, arousing.

"You should choose me because I am leader of men, future king—" he said.

"Ah, a king amongst men," she repeated. "Anything else?"

Kyran nodded. "I can provide wealth, power, and I have proven myself a warrior. I can protect you, hunt for you—"

She tossed her head back and laughed, cutting him off. "You're awfully sure of yourself, aren't you, cowpoke?"

"Yes, I am, m'lady. My word of honor has never been questioned."

This statement only made her laugh harder. "Fine, cowman, fine. I believe you. Now enough talking. It's overrated anyway. I want to dance."

The music changed and she swayed her hips seductively to the beat. Kyran didn't move. He watched his future wife dance, confident that she was dancing for his pleasure alone. This was good. Things were accepted between them. They would be married. One night in the bridal tent, a little bonding, and it would be done.

Kyran grinned. This was much better than trying to steal an unwilling woman while she kicked and screamed to be free. Maybe finding brides on Earth wouldn't be so difficult after all.

CHAPTER FOUR

Eve grabbed her head and tried not to groan, refusing to open her eyes. Tequila shots with Paul had been a bad idea—a very bad idea. She felt like her eyeballs were about to explode out of her head. Part of her wished they would. Maybe then they wouldn't hurt so much.

Only on her birthday did she let herself go wild like that. Hey, once a year wasn't bad when living in the bar scene.

Her body was stiff and she suspected she was in need of a bath. She doubted she was up to finding one anytime soon. Though, curiously, she noticed there wasn't the awful taste in her mouth—the cottonmouth sensation that came from too much partying. Had she brushed? Her mouth tasted like mint. Keeping her eyes closed, she decided it was a mystery best solved later. She would first try to fall back asleep. Just as she was on the edge of darkness once more, a sound penetrated her brain—birds singing. That's when she noticed the smell of nature and the cool breeze brushing over her skin.

Birds?

Nature?

In the city?

What the...?

Her eyes popped open. She was in a large red tent. There was a basin filled with water in the corner in front of her. Sitting up, she glanced around. Light streamed in from outside and a breeze came through a narrow flap. The tent was pyramid shaped and there was a large bed in the middle of the fur-covered ground.

Eve tensed as she felt the bed shift. Biting her lip, she looked to the side to find an incredibly gorgeous man next to her. Black, shoulder-length hair was tousled over his broad shoulders and she couldn't make out his face. He breathed softly in sleep, his back rising and falling in even tempo.

His *naked* back. And naked arms. And naked hips and ass. And naked—*everything*.

In light of her circumstances, Eve did the only

thing she could think of. She screamed at the top of her lungs.

The sexy man jerked, instantly on his feet as if ready to fight. She screamed again. He was huge. Bulging, oiled muscles covered every inch of him from thick neck to strong legs. There was nothing between her and his hard, bronzed flesh.

Survival instinct kicked in, and she jumped off the bed. Bright blue eyes turned to her in confusion. Eve stiffened.

Damn, but he was fucking hot.

Something tickled her flesh, drawing her attention from the sexy, god-like man. She looked down. Her body was barely covered in a fine gauze and silk gown. The slinky material hugged tight over the hips and flared around the legs. The low neckline revealed a generous amount of cleavage. Her feet were bare.

Who had changed her clothes? What was going on here? Surely Paul—

"I did not get your name last night, my bride," the man said. His voice sent chills over her.

Eve's eyes whipped to him. Then, seeing the tent flap, she yelled, "Paul!"

"Paul?" the man repeated. "You are called Paul?"

Eve didn't wait for him to finish before she

started running out the front flap of the tent. It was awkward trying to move while trying to conceal her barely covered body parts with her hands, but she managed to make it outside. A giant forest surrounded the tent. The trees towered high above the ground and yellow ferns spread out over the area.

"Paul, you got me," Eve screamed. "You win the prank war!"

Spinning on her heels, she hit flush against the naked man's chest. He tried to put his arms around her, but she shoved him hard. She screamed once more, loud and long, stumbling back as she swatted away his pursuit.

"I assure you, my woman, there is no need to speak so loudly. I am able to hear you quite well."

Eve made a run for the forest, only to stop as a giant blue parrot-like bird dove for her head and squawked in her face. The high-pitched sound rivaled hers. She tumbled back with another loud cry of alarm.

Two strong hands grabbed her from behind and spun her around before she could even think to catch herself. She took a deep breath, intent on screaming again, when suddenly the man kissed her. The feel of his firm, hot lips pressed tightly to hers shut her up.

Moaning weakly, she didn't pull away. Her arms

fell to her sides and she let him hold her. Every thought swam out of her head, leaving her in a sea of sweet emotions. Slowly, he moved his lips against hers, a tender caress as he tested her response to him. He edged his tongue along her lips, thrusting just inside the delicate boundary. He tasted good, like mint, and he smelled even better.

There was something familiar in the kiss, like she'd done it before. Had she been with this man the night before? Instantly, she knew they hadn't had sex. She liked to flirt with the men, but she wasn't one for a casual fling. Besides, if the huge erection pressing into her stomach was any indication, her body would definitely feel the remnants of anything he might have done to her.

He glided his hands around to the small of her back, rubbing in circles as he pulled her tighter to his frame. Hot, solid flesh molded to her, forcing her softer skin to conform to its will. Instinctively, she opened her mouth, moaning in approval for him to deepen the kiss. He did, delving his tongue deeper, exploring every inch of her mouth like he couldn't get enough. It felt so good. He tasted like a potent drug she wanted to drink more of. Eve couldn't remember ever being kissed with so much passion, so much desire. She would have to be dead not to respond to it.

She lifted up on her toes, deepening an already searing kiss as her lungs burned for air. Her hands traveled up his arms to his shoulders. He cupped her ass, lifting her off the ground with little effort. The strength in him scared and exhilarated her at the same time. Her heart beat hard and heavy, pumping her desire like a shockwave through her body. He crushed his erection against her lower stomach, making it clear what he wanted from her. Then something he'd said struck her. Did he call her his bride?

Eve gasped, pulling back, fighting the drug-like daze that threatened her senses. Her limbs were numb with desire and heat. His bright blue eyes peered into hers. They were startling in their brilliant color. Part of her wanted to forget reason and keep going. Part of her wanted to beg him to take her right there on the strange fern-covered ground, there under the peculiar green-tinted sky.

"Much better, m'lady," the man said, nodding. He kept her body tight against his, holding her as if she were a feather. She detected every subtle movement of him. His firm lips brushed forward and she pulled back, just out of his reach. He nipped playfully at the air, and said, "I like that I can calm you in such a way."

"Did you...?" Eve swallowed nervously. "Did you call me...? Where are we? What happened last night? Didn't you have sideburns?"

"Do you really want to talk now?" His bright eyes were full of sexual meaning and promise. "Can we not talk after?"

"After what?" Eve played dumb.

"You have to ask?" He pressed lightly into her with his erection. "I've been waiting all night for you. You fell asleep before we could finish what we started during your dance."

Eve pushed at his shoulders and took a deep breath. The memory of boldly making out with him on the dance floor filtered through her mind. She'd seen him from the stage, had found him later at the bar with his foreign money. She'd drummed up the nerve to talk to him, actually considered him a birthday present to herself. Had she really jumped on him like that while they were on the dance floor? Wrapping her arms around his neck and her legs around his waist? Had she really begged him to take her back to his hotel room? How much tequila did she drink? "I was dosed, wasn't I? Damn it. It's gotten to the point you can't even go out anymore."

Even as she said it, she knew it wasn't true. Her wanton actions had been one-hundred percent embarrassingly her. She pushed harder and he let her go. Her feet dropped on the ground and she stumbled.

"Dosed?"

Eve ignored his confusion. She stepped away from him, suddenly feeling chilled though the air was warm. It was really bright out and she glanced at the cloudless sky. Was she mistaken, or were there three suns overhead—two yellow and a very pretty blue one?

"I'm on acid," she stated, continuing away from the strange guy. She stared at him, relieved that he'd wrapped a linen piece of material around his waist to hide his morning nakedness. "I remember you. You're the cowboy who wasn't dancing. You came to my show with a bunch of your friends all dressed up. You must've slipped something into my drink. Oh, no. You're a kidnapper, aren't you?"

"No, I am Draig. Don't you remember me telling you this last night? My name is Kyran—"

Eve held up her hand, moaning in protest. "Uh, no. I don't want to hear it. The less I know about you the better. Just let me go home and I'll forget I even saw you. Okay?"

"You can't go home. You don't remember the portal? Coming to my planet?"

"Planet?" she squeaked, breathing hard. She fanned her face. Did he just say planet?

"Yes, Qurilixen. Do you need me to kiss you again? You look..." He shrugged, helpless.

"Oh, oh, you're crazy. You think you're...alien... spaceship..." Eve couldn't catch her breath as panic gripped her, "...crazy...probing...mental hospital...crazy..."

"Hold, easy—"

"Don't you tell me to take it easy, you lunatic!" she yelled, still gasping for breath. "You kidnapped me and brought me out to the forest. You psycho, there are laws against this. You can't just take people out of Cleveland when they want to be in Cleveland!"

"Are you well?" He arched a brow.

"Bloody hell! No, I'm not well. I've been abducted by a crazy lunatic who thinks he's an alien. You've taken me against my will and made me see suns."

At that, he actually looked upset. "No, I told you I chose you and you accepted."

"I accepted that you were from Quasar and

agreed to be beamed to your planet? Not bloody likely! I don't care how much tequila I drank."

"Yes, though it's called Qurilixen, not Quasar."

"Wonderful. You're an alien. Why not?" Eve wondered if she was insane. "I'm going to be one of those crazies talking about probing and tracking implants while making aluminum foil suits."

"I do not consider myself an alien," he said thoughtfully. "However, I do suppose from you point of view that is technically correct, though we did not fly through space to get here. And my people did originate on your planet many, many years ago."

"Not an alien. Then what are you, portal man?"

"A dragon-shifter." He looked serious. "What is with all this bloody you speak of? I don't understand the phrase."

"I picked it up from a British guitarist who let me crash on her couch after...*argh.* Quit trying to change the subject!" He didn't look pleased by her tone. Eve didn't care. She wasn't pleased either, being in the middle of the woods with a nutcase. "You took me against my will. Now I demand you tell me how to get home. Right now!"

She stomped her foot for effect. He didn't look too impressed by the action as he adjusted the material at his waist. The man hardly acted like he wanted to hurt her. In fact, he just looked horny and confused.

"You dare to question my honor? I am Kyran of the Draig. No one has ever dared to question my honor." He took a deep, harsh breath. His fists clenched and unclenched at his sides in anger. Between his teeth, he growled, "You said, fine, cowboy, fine. I believe you. Now enough talking. It's overrated anyway. I want to dance."

"*What?* From that you got, take me to your alien planet, you big stud?" She shook from head to toe. "Just stay away from me. I'm warning you."

"Warning me of what?" He glanced around the forest. "There is nothing here to be afraid of."

"Just stay back!"

"Back where?"

"Stop that!"

"Stop what?"

"Shut up! Just stay back! Don't move." Eve glanced around. Where should she go? All she saw was trees and his giant red, pyramid tent. The only sound was the flapping of the top blue banner whipping on the breeze. It had a silver dragon in the middle of it—very medieval in design. "Are you an actor? Did someone pay you to do this? Did Paul...?"

Damn, why did he have to be so attractive? It

made it really hard to concentrate—especially when he had kissed her all soft and tender like he had.

What the hell was wrong with her? Who cared if the crazy man looked good naked? She kept waiting for a sign he meant to harm her but didn't find one. There was arrogance in his expression, but no malice.

"Pay me to marry you?" Kyran tilted his head, looking adorably confused. "No, I accepted no dowry—"

"Ah." Eve tried to remain calm, but it was hard. There were three freaking suns over her head. "Married? Did you just say married?"

"Yes, we are married. Last night, when you stayed with me in my tent."

"I passed out. I didn't technically stay anywhere."

"You are my princess," he said, his tone harder than before. His face and stance dared her to deny it.

"Princess? Oh, that's great. Princess Eve and Prince Kyran. All right then. Whatever. You win. I'm a princess and we're on your home planet. Now where is this portal at? I have a gig tonight. I promise to be home by dinner, darling." Eve tried to smile, but she knew the expression was strained. Okay, time to ditch Mr. Crazypants. Only where was she going to go? She knew nothing about wilderness survival. Nearing her breaking point, she mumbled, "That's it. I've gone mad. That nun told me my party lifestyle would catch up with me and it has. I'm mental. You're not real. That tent's not real. Nothing's real."

"Are you—"

"No, no, I don't need you to kiss me again. Once was enough, trust me." Eve turned her back on him and tried to walk away. Seeing a small gathering, she stopped. "Oh, great. There are more of you."

CHAPTER FIVE

KYRAN WATCHED his bride in puzzlement. She was acting stranger than the night before. What was wrong with her? Last night she'd seemed all into him, and now she was screaming that awful noise at every turn. He really hoped she didn't continue to do so every morning. His ears would never grow used to it. At first, he'd thought it was simply an Earth custom, until he'd seen the panic on her face.

His bride was scared. For that he was sorry. Though kissing her had seemed to calm her a great deal. Her heart had sped, but with a different beat than before. If a kiss was all it took, he'd gladly keep her the most placated of maids.

He looked over her tight backside in the traditional gown of the Draig people. The waist-wrap he wore and her gown were merely for the wedding ceremony. Kyran would be the first to admit that his wedding had been anything but traditional. However, dressing his bride in her wedding clothes had been a particular treat. It had afforded him a great view of what was to be his to enjoy.

Her breasts were perfect handfuls, so soft with large dark nipples that puckered under the slightest touch—not that he'd touched her more than necessary when she was sleeping. She'd been awake when she'd taken off her clothes, moaning softly for more kisses.

He'd been pleased to discover the hair between her thighs didn't look to be blue—though he wasn't completely positive as he hadn't removed the small article of clothing covering her hips. She'd fallen asleep naked and so he'd dressed her. It had been hard though, especially after watching her dance for him at the *club*—as they called the noisy place he'd found her in. It was a fitting name since the sounds coming from the music boxes had pounded him in the head like an invisible club.

Seeing his parents gathered with Finn and the two Var princes along the edge of the forest, he held up his hand. The king and queen looked worried. It was no wonder, with his bride screaming like she was.

His mother, Queen Galina, wore a two-layer purple gown. The fitted undertunic was a light cream color. The dark purple overtunic's sleeves were long, belling around the elbows, and the snug waist fanned into a long skirt. Silver embroidery edged the gown in an intricate Qurilixian pattern, and on the bodice, in the center of the chest, was their family emblem of the dragon.

Though Kyran liked the outfit his wife wore very much, part of him desired to see her dressed as a fine lady—befitting her new station. His mother had already agreed to help his bride with her wardrobe and anything else she might require.

A band of gold wrapped around his mother's head. She only wore the crown for ceremonies, and today was considered one of the most blessed for their people. It was his first day of being mated—the first of many days if he would be so favored by the gods.

His father, King Severin, and Finn wore a simpler garment. His brother was in dark blue and the king in purple to match the queen. They had tunics with the same silver-embroidered edges and a larger patch on the center of their chests. The tunic was more of a long shirt that split at the sides than an actual dress. The two Var princes were clothed as Ivar had been the night before—in breeches and shirts with cross laces down the center of their chests. The styles difference had a lot to do with how the races shifted. Draigs could shift and remained clothed. The Var could shift partially into a man-cat or completely into full cats. Cat-shifters needed to part with their clothing at a moment's notice. The Draig tended to be more reserved than their beastly counterparts.

"What is all this noise, son?" King Severin asked in their native tongue. His bride blinked, glancing back at him. Seeing her fear, he felt sorry for her. The urge to protect what was his became strong. Slowly, he came forward, watching her to make sure she didn't try to run. Although, if she did, he'd easily be able to shift to his Draig form and catch her.

Once the idea entered his head, he had a hard time dismissing it immediately. That wasn't such a bad idea. He wondered if his bride would like being hunted. The warrior inside him stirred. If he didn't get her alone and naked soon, he'd burst.

"It is nothing, my king," he said, keeping his

words in the language his bride could understand. "Queen Galina, King Severin, may I present Lady Eve of the Earthen people. My princess and soon to be yours."

Eve didn't move, save to sway on her feet. A soft noise left her. It sounded suspiciously like a snort.

His mother stepped forward. Her voice was gentler than her husband's and she spoke in words Eve could understand. "Welcome to the family of Draig, Lady Eve. I wish you much happiness and a blessed marriage."

"Many blessings, m'lady," the others agreed in unison.

"Come, dear," Galina said, motioning with her hand. "You must be exhausted. Let me show you to the palace."

Eve didn't move. Galina waited a moment before lowering her hand. She glanced at her son in confusion. Kyran nodded for them to go so he could be alone with his bride. He saw the hurt in the queen's eyes but could do nothing about that now. Galina knew, as did they all, that the human brides would need time to adjust.

"Eve?" he asked when they were again alone.

She didn't speak.

"I like your name. It's very pretty."

"Don't move. It will all go away."

"What will go away?" he asked, concerned. She was acting strange. In truth he wasn't sure what was considered strange for her.

"Don't answer. He'll disappear, like the others just did."

"Eve?"

"I am not an alien princess," she said, finally looking at him. "And you are not my incredibly hot new husband."

At that Kyran quirked a brow. "Hot?"

"See, if this was real, you'd have two heads or suction-cup fingers or antennas or something. You look human. And logic would dictate that the chances of two like lifeforms evolving on two different planets were...you know, not likely. So there, I reasoned it out. You can go away now. The acid trip is over."

"You wish to see our differences? I can show you, but I have no way of knowing how you'll react to it. I'm told by the scouts that the shift can be frightening for Earthlings."

"Oh, no," she said, her tone dry as she waved her arms to the side. "Please, by all means, show me how we're different. But I'm warning you. Just pulling down your pants and showing me that you have a willy isn't going to work. I've seen naked men before."

Kyran tensed. "You speak of other men to me? Your past is your past, but you dare to mention it? Now? On this day?"

Eve trembled, flinching as he reached for her. He pulled back.

"Oh, yeah, Kyran. I've had boyfriends. Lots of big, studly boyfriends. We had sex, lots and lots of sex in every position you could ever imagine. I've been ridden more times than a—"

"Very well, bride, it will be as you wish. I will show you how we are different."

Kyran's skin hardened as it turned a dark brown. A line grew out from his forehead, pushed forward to make a hard plate of impermeable tissue over his nose and brow. His eyes yellowed, able to see down to every microscopic movement of her body. Talons grew from his nail beds as deadly fangs extended from his gums. His dragon-like nostrils flared as he studied her.

"Maybe now you see why you should not upset me with your lies, m'lady." His voice was hoarse with the transformation.

He waited for her to scream. Instead, she stared at him for a long time. Then, weakly, she whispered, "Yep. That would make you an alien all right."

Kyran reached for her with lightning reflexes, just in time to catch her before she hit the ground. Sighing, he lifted her limp body easily into his arms. What an unusual way to begin their mated life together.

CHAPTER SIX

A SEXY MAN who turned into a dragon-like beast? Alien planet? Three suns? Yep. It was decided. Eve was never drinking again.

She slowly opened one eye, hesitantly looking through a narrow slit. There was no red tent. That was something. However, the gray stone wall was little better. Groaning, she opened the second eye. "Where in the world am I now?"

The bed was enormous, carved from dark wood. It was the biggest she'd ever seen, raised up on a stone platform and reached by steps at the end. A barren fireplace dominated most of the wall in front of her. Its mantel was empty, but there was a large dark blue banner with a silver dragon hanging over it. The dragon matched the one embroidered on the bedspread covering her. Throw pillows at the end of the bed were opposite in color—silver with dark blue dragons. She tossed the bedspread aside and found that she no longer wore the strange gauzy outfit, but now a long cotton nightdress that looked as if it belonged on her great-great-grandmother.

"Okay, the dragon man I can handle," she mumbled, "but who keeps changing my clothes?"

The bedroom was a large rectangle with a high-vaulted ceiling like a miniature gothic cathedral. At the very top, there was a domed glass window. A long pull string hung from the middle of it. By the soft light coming from outside, she easily guessed it was daytime.

There were no doors that she could see, only arched entryways. One led to a long room with chairs and a couch. Two giant dark wood wardrobes were set along one wall opposite a narrow slit of a window. The first wardrobe was empty. Inside the second were men's clothes.

"Kyran," she whispered, touching the sleeve of a blood-red tunic edged with black. Next to the wardrobe on a low table was an array of jewelry—metal armbands, a silver and gold crown, a collection of brooches. She lifted a brooch, studying the intricate design. Glancing up, she saw an array of vicious weaponry hanging on the wall—swords, knives, axes, maces, a few things she didn't even know what to call. Her fingers shook and she dropped the brooch. "Oh, crap. I'm on a planet stuck in the medieval period. I think I'd rather be crazy."

Crossing to the narrow window, she tried to peek outside. All she saw was the tops of trees below in a valley, as if the home stood on top of a mountain.

Leaving the giant dressing room, she tried the next arch. It led to another long room with a desk and several thick chairs. Rolled parchments of paper filled wooden boxes along one wall. A blue feather quill and a jar of ink were on the desk. It appeared to be someone's office.

The third archway held an enclosed stairwell. Running her fingers over the cold stone, she walked down the dim stairwell, following the curve of the steps. The floor was cool against her bare feet. The light from above made it easy to see. She neared the bottom and hesitated.

"Hello?" she whispered. "Is anyone there?"

No answer.

Eve stepped into a large, open room, and gasped. The domed window in this section was bigger than the bedroom's and the arched ceiling seemed to spiral up toward it. A curtain covered most of it to block the majority of light. Two thick columns came down on either side of the dome. Between the columns, the floor sank into a large oval. Circular gray couches surrounded a gigantic pit fireplace in the middle. Blue throw pillows with the embroidered insignia of a dragon rested neatly on the suede-like material. The black grates in the center surround a fire that was left burning.

Kyran slept on a couch. Orange firelight framed his face and danced erotically over his flesh. A blanket covered his legs, but his arms and chest were left bare. The curve of his smooth hip teased her with what lay hidden. The sculpted muscles formed a strong stomach, the indentations like the product of an artist. Now, sleeping, his breath rising and falling, he looked very human.

Eve bit her lip. This wasn't so bad, this surreal moment standing in an alien's home. Kyran really was a handsome man. It was no wonder she'd been attracted to him from the first. She actually preferred him out of the cowboy attire. Then, blushing, she wondered if he wore the Polynesian style, plain-colored lava-lava around his waist *all* the time. Probably not. The other men had been in tunics and laced shirts.

Tiptoeing past him, she continued exploring. A

partial stone wall blocked a bathroom from view, though it technically had no door. The long bench with a hole and a lid appeared to be the toilet. She didn't see any paper, and the place didn't smell like a campground outhouse. A huge stone tub dominated the center of the room and was filled with bubbling, steaming water like a natural hot spring.

The next room was a small kitchen. It had a red stone sink with running water and a matching smooth stone countertop with the black insignia of the dragon inlaid on the top. There was a stove grate over a fire pit, a brick oven and a variety of appliances she would never know how to use. Pulling at a hatch in the floor, she felt cold air hit her. It was the refrigerator.

"We usually take our meals in the common hall, so I don't have much in here. But if you're hungry, I'm sure I can find you something."

Eve jumped at Kyran's voice and dropped the hatch. It slammed shut with a heavy thud. He stood in the door way. Her gaze automatically traveled from his bare feet up to his startling blue eyes. He wore a loose pair of linen pants and nothing else. Seeing him, so perfectly male in appearance, she was sure the dragon-shift had to have been her imagination.

When she didn't move or speak, a provocative smile curled his lips. "Or perhaps you're hungry for something else, m'lady?"

Heat flooded her cheeks and she was mortified to realize she was blushing.

"There is no need to be self-conscious." Kyran took a step toward her then stopped. "Though it pleases me that you are nervous. It means you care about pleasuring me."

Huh?

Eve stared at him, taking a moment to process his words. When they finally made it from her ears to her numbed brain, she stiffened. "Confidence is one thing, but you're bordering on arrogance."

Kyran shrugged, unconcerned.

Eve straightened. "I want to go home."

"This palace is your home, and this wing of the palace is our private quarters." His smile faded and his expression became a blank mask. "Feel free to go where you will. You are my princess. What is mine, is yours and what is yours is—"

"Still mine," Eve quipped, pushing past him.

His hand shot out and grabbed her by the upper arm. "You test my patience, my bride."

"And you test my sanity, psychopath. Now release me."

He studied her for a long, hard moment before letting go. "It's late. Go back to bed. We'll discuss this, and what is expected of you as my wife, in the morning."

"Late?" Eve glanced up to the light coming from the dome.

"Qurilixen isn't like Earth. Our three suns keep us in daylight except for one night a year when the suns align perfectly with the one moon. Right now, it's the middle of the night. If the light bothers you, pull the curtains. Now go to bed."

"You're not the boss of me. I've been on my own since I was seventeen. I don't need someone to tell me when to sleep. I happen to like sleeping during the day and being up at night." Eve suddenly remembered her band. She groaned. "Oh, great. What time is it exactly? I'm late for work. Ah, man, my guitar. How could you take me and not my guitar?"

"There is no need for you to work."

"Ew. Nice picture you're painting here, princey boy. No working, no staying up late, no guitar. Is this a castle or reform school? I mean really, do you want me to kill myself?"

At that, his face hardened into an angry mask. What was that she'd said about the dragon thing being her imagination? Yeah, Eve now saw her mistake. His

75

eyes turned to golden fire. The skin around his eyes darkened like a hard shell. She gasped, automatically jerking back. Kyran surged forward, grabbing her wrist.

"You will never threaten to take your own life," he growled. "I forbid you to kill yourself."

Eve was too scared to think of a retort. With a loud growl, he stormed toward the stairwell, pulling her behind him. She stumbled, trying to keep up and get free at the same time. They reached the top of the stairs and Kyran maneuvered her toward the bed.

Moaning weakly as tears streamed down her cheek, she tensed. If a big man like Kyran wanted to force himself on her, she wouldn't be able to stop him. Even as she thought of it, the idea of sleeping with Kyran wasn't completely repulsive. But she didn't want it like this—not angry, not by force. His aggressiveness terrified her even as it excited her. He was bold, confident and a complete pain in the ass.

"Kyran," she whispered, her voice shaking as badly as her body.

He stopped by the bed.

"Please, don't do this." It took all her willpower to get the words out. She was never one to beg, no matter what life threw at her. Still, this was one battle she couldn't win.

He took a deep, ragged breath. When he turned, his eyes were back to the brilliant blue. "I won't hurt you."

For some insane reason she couldn't name, Eve believed him. Kyran climbed onto the bed, taking her with him. She didn't protest as much as she should have. Then, lying down, he tugged her next to him and pulled up the covers. He rested on his side, slowly stroking the hair back from her brow.

"This isn't..." Eve wasn't sure what she was trying to say.

"I was going to let you have the bed but cannot remove all the weapons from this room tonight to keep you safe, so it is my duty to lie here and make sure you do not hurt yourself." He rolled onto his back and closed his eyes. "I'm a trained warrior. I will hear you if you try anything foolish. I have no wish to shackle you, but I will if that is the only way I can ensure your safety."

Eve lay on her back, watching his even breathing. She would never seriously kill herself, but apparently figures of speech weren't a big thing on this planet. His arm rested near hers and the warmth from his side soaked into her bones. She really wasn't tired, but being cared for in such an extreme way was somewhat comforting, and she found herself closing her eyes and relaxing.

Just when she was sure he was sleeping, he said quietly, "You're so soft. It's taking all my willpower not to touch you."

"You are touching me." Eve opened her eyes to look at him.

"Not as I wish to be. I would that you asked me for more." He remained still, not bothering to open his eyes to look at her reaction.

He was asking for permission?

The hazy light from above shadowed his face. She didn't need to see his features. Already she had them memorized. His body was warm against hers, heating her already aroused blood. What was it about this man? He was arrogant. He was her alien abductor. Yet, here she was, lying next to him thinking about how good his lips had felt against hers and how good he'd tasted.

Bits and pieces of their first night together filtered through her mind. Parts of it were still hazy—like actually travelling through a wormhole to another planet. However, she remembered that she had been the one to buy him a drink. She'd taken his hat. She'd made him dance with her—well, she'd danced and he'd stood like an incredibly dorky column in his cowboy getup. She'd been the one to touch him first, kiss him first, clearly emboldened by the numerous shots of tequila. In fact, if she remembered it correctly, he'd tried to resist her charms. She was the one who'd flirted with him, coming on very strong. Almost every time, she'd been the one to initiate their contact. Even now, he'd only grabbed her wrist because she'd threatened to end her own life.

Curious.

Eve had never been one to be completely freaked out by the unexplained and often surged forward into the unknown without serious thought of the consequences. Sure, she sometimes got into trouble, but she also got to experience really cool things—like ghost hunting an abandoned asylum overnight. They hadn't found evidence, but it had been exhilarating.

It was jarring thinking that aliens were real and that she was on another planet. But if she stopped and thought about it, life was all about the roller coaster ride. This was an adventure—possibly one of the biggest adventures in mankind's history. And she was on it. How many people could say the same thing? If she just accepted that what was happening was real and pushed past her own fears and doubts, where would this adventure lead?

So did she surge forward and take the chance? Or did she miss an opportunity and wonder forever what an intimate night with a man like Kyran might be like? She'd been ready to sleep with him after a night at the bar.

"Do you?" Eve shivered, glancing down his lean form. "Are you...? Is your kind, um, made to, um...?"

His chest vibrated as he suppressed a chuckle. He finally turned to look at her. "You wish to know if I am made for you?"

Eve nodded. Fear and excitement made her blood pump wildly through her veins, drowning out reason. He rolled toward her and adjusted his hips, pressing his hardened shaft to her side. The heat of it seared her through her clothing, letting her feel how very much he desired her. Not only was it like fire, it was big—a veritable weapon. Kyran leaned into her ear, licking at the lobe, "Why don't you discover the answer for yourself?"

Damn, but it was arousing to feel his erection pressing into her like it was. His hips moved in tiny thrusts, rubbing along her. She'd seen him move—the quick, agile grace of his body—and knew he was a man who'd know how to work it between the sheets.

There was passion in his tone but also an unmistakable challenge. Curiosity was definitely one of her greatest vices. Rolling on her side to face him, she trailed her hand over his hard, flat stomach. He tensed, closing his eyes as he held his breath. His navel was carved just as she'd expect to find one and his flesh was every inch hard, sizzling male. Eve got to his waistband and hesitated. He opened one eye to look at her.

"Will you change during?" she asked.

"No, we do not shift to mate." He gave a pained smile. "I have no wish for you to be frightened, m'lady. I would never harm you in this. You have my word."

Eve nodded, instinctively believing him. It was strange, but she felt the building of a connection between them. Or maybe it was just that she was so aroused by him she couldn't see straight. The ache between her thighs was nearly unbearable as her body readied to accept him.

Kyran took a deep breath. "Mm, I love your smell."

He could smell her? She clamped her thighs together on instinct. He must have felt her movement, because he again chuckled.

"Are you trying to torture me?" His voice was soft as he continued to nuzzle her ear. Pushing his hips closer, he urged her to continue her exploration.

Eve dipped her hand along his hip and angled her neck to give him access to her throat. Her neck was always so sensitive. He brushed his lips over her, giving her instant goose bumps.

"You have protection, right?" she asked.

"Yes, I will protect you," he assured her. "As is my duty to you."

Eve's hand stilled just below his waist band. "No, I mean protection. Like a condom."

"Sorry? Condom?"

Eve pulled her hand away. Her body ached in protest, but she refused to give in. "Yeah, you know, something to prevent diseases."

"You believe me to be diseased?" He actually looked insulted. "You think I would come to you in such a way?"

"Well, I don't know, maybe to prevent pregnancy. Can you even get me pregnant? Or what if your sperm is this acidy mutating stuff that has some weird effect on me?" Eve shrugged. Okay, the last one could have been the influence of too many old horror movies, but still...

Kyran rolled off the bed in one swift motion. His hair was beautifully disheveled about his head and he was breathing hard. Damn, he was even sexier pissed —if such a thing were even possible.

"Are you saying you have no wish to carry my sons?" he demanded.

Eve was taken aback. "What? Are you serious?"

"Why would I not be serious? This is a serious matter. You are my wife. It is your duty to have my sons."

"What? No girls?" she asked wryly. Was this man for real? The way she saw it, if he was this crazy there was no point in trying to talk reason.

His face fell. "I can't give you daughters."

That wasn't the answer she'd been expecting.

"For some reason, since my people escaped to this planet from yours, we have slowly stopped producing female children. I tell you this because you should know, but I ask that you do not speak of it freely to our people. They have noticed the decline in female births, but we have not made the extent of the problem known."

Eve nodded. What else could she do?

"Don't be concerned for your safety," he continued. "Live females are not adversely affected by being here."

Eve merely stared at him and he just kept talking his crazy.

"It is why we returned to Earth after so long to

find brides. I have been the first so blessed. We know your kind breeds successfully with ours."

"So I'm just something you can knock up?" Eve gave a derisive snort. "Well, jeez, when you say it like that."

"I will never knock you. You are my wife—"

Grimacing, she held up her hand, "Yeah, about that one..."

He stiffened.

"You see, I'm not sure I agree with you on the whole me-being-your-wife issue."

"But...just now, you..." He ran his hand through his hair. For a moment, she wasn't sure if he wanted to strangle her or throw her down the stairs. Either way, it didn't look good. She recoiled on the bed. To her amazement, he restrained his temper. "You are my wife."

"Just because you say it, doesn't make it so."

"No, Draig law makes it so. You willing walked into my tent. There are witnesses. You spent the night and were introduced to the king and queen the next morning. It is done."

With a heavy sigh, she rested on her back and said nonchalantly, "Then undo it."

"Does your honor mean so little to you that you would take back your word?"

Honor? That was his defense? Eve laughed. "I don't know when the last time you've been to Earth was, but things have changed, princey."

"You will call me m'lord, lord husband, prince, my prince or Kyran. Nothing else."

"Okay, *Kyran*," she stressed his name to the point that it was hardly respectful. "Undo it."

"I will not!"

"Then I will," she quipped. Somehow, Eve instinctively knew he wouldn't harm her, no matter how mouthy she got. "What do I have to do? Sleep outside the tent?"

"No." A small smile formed on his face. "You have to petition the royal council."

There was something in his look. "As in the king and queen?"

He nodded.

"As in your parents, right?"

He nodded again. "Yes, my parents and other elders. You should also know that marriage disputes can only be claimed after a full year of marriage has been achieved and only if the bride can prove that nothing of a sexual nature happened between the married couple for that full year. Furthermore, a decision usually takes another year to be reached, considering the royal council will not always agree and the dissolution of a marriage is a very serious matter to us. So, accordingly, you have at least two years as my wife." He rubbed his chin thoughtfully. "However, if I were to disagree with the divorce, then it would be longer. We could drag this out say ten, fifteen years. Even then, you need the royal council's consent. So you see, it's not likely you can undo your word as easily as you'd like. We take our honor very seriously."

"You're on the royal council, aren't you?" She wanted to groan.

"As are my brothers and uncles and cousins."

"Ah, glad to see your honor includes fairness," she grumbled.

"Question my honor again and I'll—"

"What, break your word and actually hurt me?" Eve dismissed, sitting up with a superior smile. "Go ahead. Take your best shot. I'd like to have this honor conversation again afterward though."

"I don't have to hurt you to punish you, wife."

Part of her really wanted to forget this intriguing debate and invite him back to bed. Her gaze roamed down over his deliciously firm body. Why did she have to ask about protection before she was able to explore him more fully? She wondered if he'd be bumpy all over when he shifted. And why wasn't she put off by the idea?

"I think I see a suitable punishment already," he said. "I won't mate with you until you say the words I am your wife and you are my prince."

Eve's gaze flew up from his groin to stare at his face. "Are you serious?"

"Extremely." His eyes flickered with gold.

There was that challenge again. Damn, but she was a fool. She was going to take his challenge and issue one of her own. Eve tilted her head to the side. "Good to know, but I'm not so sure I'll be the one to cave first."

Standing on the bed, she pulled her nightgown over her head and tossed it aside. She posed before him in nothing but her lace panties. Kyran's eyes devoured her and his lips parted as he sucked in a deep breath. The gold only increased in intensity as he stared.

"By the way, I like to walk around the house naked. I hope that won't be a problem." Eve gave him a superior grin, reaching to absently rub the bottom curve of her breasts. His eyes automatically followed her movement as if mesmerized.

Men are so easy, she thought.

"Well, marriage is about compromises, wife. I am

willing to learn some of your customs as well. Besides, I too find clothes to be rather binding."

She knew what was coming even before he pushed his loose-fitted pants off his hips. Eve stared at his towering shaft. It was full, and so impossibly thick with need. Aside from the size, he looked every inch human. His perfect hips framed it, leading to strong thighs and calves. He kicked his pants aside, letting her look her fill.

"I'm assuming you have maids here? I know you don't think I'm picking up after you." Eve nodded pointedly to his discarded pajama pants and yawned.

"No, the servants will see to it. But I must insist you wear more than those hip coverings when they are around. Otherwise, it is a punishable offense and I would be able to do little to save you from it."

"Great. Good to know. Though it is a shame that I have to take streaking off my list of things to do on this planet while I'm here." She hopped off the bed, not at all tired. It was night after all—her time to be awake. "I'm hungry. I'm going to go get some food and then take a nice long, hot, wet bath."

As she said the words, she let her voice dip with meaning and then bit her lip, giving him her most seductive naughty-girl look. Always the adventurer, she had no problem standing before him in her underwear. Besides, this hunky alien prince was just too delicious for words.

Kyran drew his hands up to his hips, pausing to scratch below his navel. "I must rest. A prince's day is very full."

"Sweet dreams." Eve waited for him to break first and give into his desire for her. The electricity between them was so alive it nearly snapped in the air. They were both breathing hard. The subtle scent of arousal was thick. Every nerve in her body was ready for some action.

"M'lady." Kyran bowed his head in dismissal and walked to the bed. "You know where to find me when you are ready to accept me as your husband and master."

Eve snorted and walked down the stairs in her lace panties. She paused, listening to see if he would follow. He didn't. Almost pissed that he'd resisted her, she stomped to the kitchen.

"Damn, barbaric alien..." She continued mumbling, cursing as she went in search of something decent to eat.

KYRAN LAY ON THE BED, his body taut. Every inch of him was aroused even though the woman frustrated the dragonfire out of him. He listened to her walk down the stairs, his Draig senses so in tune with her that he knew she stopped and waited. He detected her lingering scent. The hunter inside him stirred and primal instinct warred with his logical mind. Did he give into his natural urges and take her? Even as he wanted to, he knew that for the sake of their future together, he must wait for her to give into him.

Groaning, he didn't try to resist his body's needs as he reached down to grab his erection. It was so sensitive it actually hurt to stroke. But soon he was pumping his fist over the turgid shaft, working his way to a bittersweet release as he imagined a naked, wet, bathing Eve in her hip coverings.

CHAPTER SEVEN

Eve moved down the stone hallway. After the spa bath, she felt much better—even if the only thing she could find to wear was a long dress. As illogical as it sounded, the most believable explanation for her current predicament was that this was not a time slip, or alien abduction, or parallel world, so much as a kind of undiscovered country crossed to by a scientifically explainable magical portal. The dragon-shifters used to live on her side of the portal, which is why myths of dragons and shapechangers still existed on her world. They'd left. People had forgotten about them. And now they'd rediscovered their way back across the space ocean like Europeans of old sailing to the supposedly New World.

Some people evolved with dark or light skin and

biological features according to their environment. Kyran's people had evolved into human dragons. The proof of their Earth past was evident in the fact she was walking through a medieval castle. Thinking of this place as a foreign country made it a lot easier to accept. She would simply have to navigate the local customs and laws until she found a way home.

"Hey, better a portal than a space ship," she mumbled, peeking around a corner. Any idiot could jump into a portal—she assumed it was something you could jump into—but there was no way she was flying a space ship. She could barely drive stick shift in a car.

Giving up on sneaking around, since no one seemed to be awake anyway, she started wandering the long halls looking for a front door. It was by dumb luck that she found the way out. A large barred gate with metal spikes along the bottom edge had been left open. It hung overhead so she could pass under. Beyond that, two oversized wooden doors were open to let a cool breeze in. Only too late did she see the two guards standing watch. They glanced at her but made no move to stop her as she came toward them.

Eve smiled. "Good evening, fello—"

Her face collided with what looked like empty air but felt like a giant electrical shock. It zapped her hard, forcing all her muscles to stiffen violently before she was flung backwards to the hard floor. Seconds before her body struck, she thought, *Oh, fuck.*

"You should have been watching her," Queen Galina said, not for the first time. She pointed to the unconscious Eve in the palace's hospital bed.

Kyran averted his eyes to avoid his mother's irritated gaze. She was one of the last female dragons born and her fiery temper ran hotter than any male dragon-shifter. Normally it took a lot to get her angry. Apparently, one of those things was having her new daughter-by-marriage electrocuted by the guard shield.

"This will never do," the queen continued. "We have to come up with a better integration plan for bringing brides through the portal."

"To be fair, who walks through the main entrance to a castle without disarming a guard shield?" The king kept his voice even. He unconsciously rubbed the tip of his nose.

Kyran glanced at his bride. The tip of her nose was burnt and blistered. The doctors said she was going to be all right after her shock but expected her to be weak for a few days. What concerned them more was the way she'd hit her head when she fell. The palace guards hadn't realized what she was doing until it was too late.

This part of the palace was hardly ever in use. Aside from the occasional mishap, the nearby villagers rarely came to the palace to seek medical care. Shifters healed much more quickly than humans apparently did.

"It's not so bad," Finn said, trying to sound encouraging. "Maybe she can wear a face veil?"

The queen glared at her youngest son. "She is still beautiful and she is still a princess."

"I was being serious," Finn defended like a scolded child. "She has a skin bubble on her nose."

"I will tolerate no jests out of you. When she wakes up, if you so much as look at her nose, I will close that portal myself and you will never marry." Galina let her eyes flash with a gold shift. "And I will cancel all visiting ships."

Finn paled and looked to their father. The king did not naysay his wife. Everyone knew who the ruling force in that relationship was.

"Kyran, you need to do better," Queen Galina ordered. "We already discussed that these women would be fragile. They're not shifters." She sighed heavily and furrowed her brow in worry as she looked at the unconscious Eve. "But it is clearly worse than I feared. We will just have to enact certain laws and customs to ensure they're protected. It will take some time, but people will look to the princes on how to act. We need to lead by example from the beginning. I worry that the men will assume they are fierce like dragon women when clearly they can be broken."

It had taken the queen a long time to accept the fact that her sons would not be marrying dragon-shifters, but humans. Once she agreed to an idea, she embraced it fully.

"I will not leave her side until she is healed," Kyran promised. He thought about her threat to kill herself but did not want to tell his parents as much. If that is what she had been trying to do walking into the shield, she had almost been successful.

"It must be more than that. From now on, when-ever she is concerned, you will tell yourself that women are to be protected." The queen nodded slowly, as if convinced she knew the answer. "You will say it until you believe it. We have all read the historical scrolls about Earth and the human people. Where these non-dragon women are concerned, women are to be safeguarded at all costs." She took a deep breath, clearly not liking the decree against women but at the same time knowing that humans were not dragon-shifters. "Men provide, fight, protect. Women nurture, care and provide a steady household."

"Like the Victorians from the transmission documents," Finn offered. "Men rule the outside sphere of the world. Women rule the inside sphere of the home."

"Documentaries," the king corrected. The human's historical records had been most helpful.

"Clearly, that is how these delicate women are used to being treated," the queen agreed. "It has to be the will of the gods. I realize the answer as surely as if the gods had come down and whispered it in my ear."

"Finn, come, let's see the Var princes off. They ride for home this morning." King Severin patted Kyran's arm before leading Finn out of the palace hospital.

"You could not have known she would be so delicate," Queen Galina said to Kyran when they were alone. "The gods would not have blessed you if they did not want you to have her as your wife. Now that it is done, you cannot find another."

"I don't want another," he said. "I want Eve. Only Eve."

"It's a strange feeling, isn't it?" The queen smiled. "That connection you feel will only grow. Soon she will be a part of your soul. That is what marriage is."

CHAPTER EIGHT

"Good morning, Rudolf, all ready to lead Santa's sleigh tonight?" Eve mumbled. She stared at her nose in the mirror and gingerly poked at the tip. The blister was gone, but a scab had replaced it. She wore one of Kyran's tunic shirts with a belt around her waist to fashion a dress. The skirt hung to mid-thigh and the top was baggy. It actually didn't look half bad, and it beat the stack of renaissance faire gowns she'd been given as an alternative.

"Come." Kyran crossed over his living room so swiftly that she barely had time to gasp before he swept her up into his arms. Instantly, he started running for the front door in a panic. "Do not worry. Do not worry."

Eve caught her breath and lightly hit him on the

arm. "What the hell is wrong with you? Put me down."

He came to an abrupt stop. The man actually looked confused. "You called me Rudolf and asked if I was ready to slay for this Santa. The surgeon said to watch for signs of confusion and..."

Eve slowly shook her head. "I was talking to my nose, and I'm not crazy. Your doctors can't do anything to help me anyway."

He released her and she slid down his body to stand on her feet. "You were talking to your nose?"

"Not my nose, but my face, oh, you know what I mean." Eve covered her face with her hand. Though the wound no longer throbbed, it looked awful. He'd been caring for her since it happened—bringing her strange foods that looked like moldy bread and something that came out of the rare fruit section of the grocery store. "I'm not confused. I'm irritated, and frustrated, and I miss my guitar, and I'm not even sure why I'm still here with you. Well, except for the fact I'm *not* going on stage looking like this."

He said nothing, which was a change from his constantly reminding her that they were married.

"You've been hovering," she said, somewhat play-ful, somewhat irritated. Eve wasn't sure what she wanted out of him—well, besides a trip back through the portal. "Scared I'll escape?"

"Scared you will injure yourself," he corrected.

"How many times do I have to tell you it was an accident? I really don't want to die."

"Then what would you like to do?" He smiled meaningfully, and she knew he waited for her to say the words "I am your wife and you are my prince" so they could have sex. It was a tempting way to pass the time, but her stubborn mouth would never let the words out. He always looked at her like that, with his steamy come-hither eyes and eager expression. His breathing deepened as if he was on the verge of exploding out of his clothes like a wild beast. "Or what would you like me to fetch you?"

It took Eve all of two seconds to come up with a list. "Out of this castle. A cheeseburger. A latte. No, three lattes. My guitar. My clothes. A hair tie. Blow dryer. Fresh air. A—"

"Come. How about I take you out of the castle." Kyran seemed eager to please her as he crossed toward the bedroom and came back holding one of the my-lady gowns. "Dress."

Eve looked down at her outfit. "I am dressed."

"You are, uh—" Kyran eyed her naked legs, "—half dressed."

Eve arched a brow.

"It is customary if you are to make an appearance as a Draig Princess that you wear..." He held up the dress for her with a hopeful expression.

Eve shook her head in denial.

"Whereas I have enjoyed your indecent display here in our home, I cannot allow other men to see your legs so exposed."

Eve crossed her arms over her chest.

"They will get the wrong impression."

Eve tilted her head to the side. "If the sight of my naked legs is going to inflame your people, then that's on them, not me." Before he could defend the Draig honor, as it looked like he was about to, she added, "However, I will compromise. Get me a pair of those pants and I'll wear them."

Eve knew not to push her attitude too far. If she wasn't careful, she might not be let out of his home. But she also wasn't the type of woman to bend her personality to fit others. She was who she was.

When he didn't answer right away, she said, "Need I remind you that you stole me from my planet. I get that a portal trip is probably like crossing the street between two places, but at the same time, it's a whole freaking other planet. I think I'm being a pretty good sport about this. Most women would be freaking out right now, crying and talking nonsense. But not me. I'm holding it together pretty well, I think. So, in light of that, I'm thinking if I want to wear a pair of freaking pants then you should let me have my freaking pants."

What started as a reasonable tone ended in near hysteria.

"You are right. I will find you pants." Kyran nodded and disappeared out the front door.

Eve sighed. Well, maybe she wasn't handling this as well as she wanted to believe.

KYRAN HELD the pants for his bride in one hand as he strode into his father's royal office. The king looked up at his approach. "Is the princess well?"

Kyran nodded. "I believe so."

"That is a relief." The king motioned that he should sit. "What brings you to my office?"

Kyran obeyed the silent gesture. "We did not go about this bride thing right. I do not think women are still used to being stolen as they once were."

"Some adjustment is to be expected."

"It is more than that. She keeps asking for things that I do not have—her Earth clothes and something called a cheeseburger, which I recall from the mini shows as being a giant food that women enjoy eating half naked very slowly." Kyran thought of Eve's beautiful legs. He would very much enjoy getting her a cheeseburger.

"Are you asking for permission to reopen the portal?"

Kyran nodded.

"We cannot open the portal so that you may find food for your bride when she has food here. The timing must be right. The humans cannot know we visit them, and our shifters cannot know the portal works as often as it does. Traffic through must be regulated."

"What are you not telling me?" Kyran asked.

"We've had reports that there is a faction of Var who do not want us to open the portal. They feel that having the portal on Draig land gives us too much power over the fate of the planet. Some feel that your being the first to marry is proof of this." King Severin frowned. "Right now, the people are still awaiting word about your princess. The next step is to make that happen. This must be done right, and it must be done fast. A cat-shifter must go next. One by one, the other princes will find wives. Then we will set a date to let the next batch of men go through."

Kyran knew the plan. He'd helped come up with the plan. "What did you tell the people?"

"That the new princess is adjusting and being monitored closely for the safety of all shifters. The surgeon issued a report as to her compatibility but fragility. The last part was your mother's doing. She is determined that all know these women are not as strong as dragon females and are to be protected."

"I think it is time that the people saw Princess Eve for themselves," Kyran said. "I'm taking her outside the palace to the village."

"She is ready?" the king asked surprised.

"Yes. Perhaps." He sighed and stood from his chair. "I hope so. We need this to work. I fear the longer we keep her locked away, the more rumors will be circulated. Once they see she is shaped well, it will put many of the men's minds at ease."

"The men are eager to find wives," the king agreed. "This plays in our favor."

"I was also thinking about the portal trips. What if we planned on making the one night of darkness the sacred marriage day? It will limit the crossing over to once a year. We can take an equal number of Var and Draig, and we can institute a palace celebration to see the men off. We'll imply that it has been discovered that travel during the night is less likely to

MICHELLE M. PILLOW

harm the females. It's true enough. If they come over when it is dark it is less likely they will be shocked by the full view of their surroundings. Eve kept mumbling about our three suns for hours."

Unless they drank tequila first. Then they apparently didn't remember the trip over...or the fact that Eve's hand had been firmly on his ass when they'd come through.

"I'll mention it to the queen." The king turned his attention back down to his desk. "You can stop avoiding taking your wife out in public now. All this can be discussed later."

Kyran bowed out of habit, even though his father wasn't looking directly at him, and left the office. The king was right. He was nervous taking his bride before his people.

CHAPTER NINE

"You should not denounce our marriage," Kyran instructed. His wife wore his tunic shirt along with the new addition of the tight pants he'd found for her. "The people won't understand."

Eve arched a brow and stared at him. He hated that look and wished she'd say something.

"They will address you as a princess," he explained. "You must allow them to."

"Kyran, do I look like an idiot?" She placed her hands on her hips.

By all the dragon's fire, she made his heart race. Every part of him wanted to touch her, be with her, please her—from his body to his mind. How could she not feel it? The attraction between them had been strong since the first moment he'd seen her on stage. When dragons mated, it was forever. He knew that she was his wife as surely as he knew he breathed air. How could she not know it?

"Because you've repeated yourself three times now. I got it. You are asking me to behave, and at this point I'll agree just so we can get out the door already." Eve nodded toward the front door.

"You act as if you have been kept prisoner in here. The door is never locked."

"Um," she pointed at her face, "you saw what happened when I went out alone. I don't really feel like being hit with an invisible hammer next time or falling into a dungeon through an invisible hole in the floor."

"That would be a ridiculous security feature," he dismissed.

"A few days ago, I would have said an invisible electric wall was ridiculous." Eve scrunched up her nose. "And now I look like a crypt keeper."

"You look beautiful," he assured her.

Eve's stern expression broke and she gave a small laugh. "They really do train you guys full out with the husband manual, don't they?"

"I don't know what that means, but if you keep smiling, I will agree with it," he said.

Eve laughed harder. He liked the sound of her

laugh. She tugged his arm. "Now let's *go*. I want to see things."

Kyran obliged, leading her through the halls. Only when she reached the front gate did she hesitate. Kyran pushed a stone and the transparent wall tinted with blue. He reached his hand through to show her it was harmless. She took cautious steps as they walked outside.

The day was warm and the green tint of the suns reflected off her hair to turn the blue streak a more vivid hue. He found the color did not disturb him as it once had—mainly because he'd noticed the hair closer to her head grew as a normal shade.

Kyran automatically started leading her toward the trees, finding it hard to fight the urge to get her alone. However, Eve detected the rooftops of the nearby village and began excitedly pulling him that way.

"Do they walk around like dragons?" she asked, practically bouncing as she walked.

"If the occasion calls for it."

"So, is it like the wolfman where you have to have a full moon to change? Or is it more of a temper thing —like letting the dragon loose where you go all mindless and start attacking people? Or is it—"

"I don't know what you're asking me. We shift if

we want to shift, if there is danger, if we fall from a great height and need to land with minimal injury to our internal organs."

"Fall?" She frowned in obvious disappointment. "So you don't fly?"

"Only females and only at very rare times."

"Oh." She sounded dejected. "So I guess you don't breathe fire?"

"There is a legend that females can when properly provoked. I have never seen it done."

Eve chuckled. "Yeah, we have that same legend amongst my people. We call it PMS."

"I have not heard of this." Kyran was glad that she seemed more at ease. "You must tell me about it."

"Oh, if I'm here long enough, I'm sure you'll learn all about it," she mumbled. Then, becoming excited once more, she said, "Hey, so if I stay here, will I turn into a dragon? Will you have to bite me like a vampire or werewolf? Or is there some kind of mystical ceremony where I drink from the goblet of dragon ooze? Or—"

"You are human," he explained very carefully. "You will remain human."

Eve's expression fell. "Well, that kind of sucks."

For some reason, her desire to become a shifter pleased him. "You no longer seem worried about being here. This pleases me. You will make a very fine queen someday, and I'm sure your new people will come to love you."

This did not seem to please her as he had hoped.

"Oh, I don't know about that." She gave him a sheepish smile before narrowing her eyes. Eve pointed toward the tree line. "Is someone watching us?"

He turned not seeing anyone.

"Never mind, he's gone. Hey, let's not get into that whole marriage thing again. You seem a decent enough sort, and heavens know I've had crazier friends."

"You will miss these other friends," he said, desiring that she know he understood the sacrifice she made. "For that I am sorry."

"My bandmates? Yes, they were a good fit for me. I'm sure they'll find someone else to hang with though. We'd only been playing together for three months. The sad truth is I doubt they'll even look for me that long."

"I am pleased you are accepting your role as my bride." He smiled and lifted his arms to touch her. This was it. Finally...

"I didn't say that," Eve corrected.

"But you accept that you are here. I thought—"

"Come on, cowboy. Enough talking. I want to see the sights." Eve jogged ahead of him down a worn foot trail, giving him no choice but to follow behind.

I AM your wife and you are my prince.

Eve knew what he wanted her to say. The challenge hung between them every time they stood in the same vicinity. Her body tingled when he was near, as if begging her to remember the familiar press of his against it. Oh, but she did remember, in raw, hot, blood-boiling, sex-wetting detail. But desire did not equal marriage. In fact, Eve had never really considered marriage as a possibility. The thought of it terrified her more than the idea of breathing alien air.

The mountains surrounded them, tall spikes reaching toward the heavens. Fresh air carried the scent of grasses and vanilla. A community surrounded the stone castle—small cottages and stretches of farmland. It was much like she'd picture an English village would look like, all nestled and cute, yards tucked behind stone walls and cobblestone paths. People took care of their property. The roads were clean.

A strange birdcall sounded, drawing her attention upwards. She blinked, instantly regretting looking toward two of the suns. Red blurs darted through the sky, flying erratically before diving into the nearby forest.

The planet was similar to Earth—well, Earth prior to the Industrial Revolution to be sure. No cityscapes and electrical light poles marred the view. The sky was clear of airplanes and industrial smokestacks. The surrounding nature was different enough that she couldn't forget she was on an alien world. The skinny trees looked like trees of the high mountains but for the bark that had a strange bubbly texture. Thick bushes with dots of yellow and bubble-bark trees filled the distant landscape.

She was surprised to find the commoners dressed like Kyran—in pants and tunic shirts. The only notable difference of rank was the dragon symbol on Kyran's chest.

When several people looked up from they were doing, Eve stopped walking. "Wait. Should you go get bodyguards or something? Is it safe for you to be out and about without protection?"

"You are concerned for my body?" He smiled and his eyes flashed golden. That little trait wasn't fair as it was all too seductive.

"You're incorrigible."

"If that means I want to see you naked, then yes, I am incorrigible."

The sound of gruff laughter cut off her answer, which was probably for the best since she didn't know what her answer was going to be. A small group of dragon men walked in from a nearby field. She noted the dirt covering their hands when they lifted them in greeting. Eve didn't understand a thing they said in their gravelly voices.

"Eve," one of the larger men repeated when Kyran introduced her. Eve's name sounded like a painful grunt.

Unsure what to do, she merely nodded her head toward him.

"Well you come," a younger dragon man said in heavily accented English, "Priceless Eve, my name is Muireadhach." He looked very proud of himself for the introduction.

"Murdock," Eve said, knowing her pronunciation probably wasn't the most flattering. "Thank you."

"Muireadhach, she is *Princess* Eve," Kyran corrected.

Eve arched a brow at Kyran and then smiled at the young man. "Priceless sounds better."

"He needs to learn the correct way," Kyran said,

his tone much more stern than it had been with her. He also looked more rigid in stance, as if the power of his position suddenly weighed down on him. "He wishes to marry and must be able to communicate with a bride before he can be chosen by the gods to go through the sacred portal."

"And this one doesn't wish to marry?" Eve asked under her breath to the one who'd growled her name.

"Beringer married one of the last dragon-shifter females before they became scarce. He sees no reason to study the language. He has his woman," Kyran said.

"Well, you speak English very well. Should I assume you were desperate to marry?" The second she said it, she wished she could take the joke back.

Kyran didn't answer. The men took their leave.

"What's that guy's story?" Eve asked, pointing at the man who kept watching them from the trees. She had detected glints of his shifting eyes as they'd gone through the village, but the second she turned her full attention to him, he'd disappear.

"Who?"

"No one," she dismissed. "He's gone now."

"Come, I will show you the rest of the village."

CHAPTER TEN

THERE WAS something very easy about being alone with the dragon prince. Eve saw the formality in him when he talked to his people, but they seemed to respect and like him in return. That genuine admiration did much to encourage her positive assessment of his character.

Kyran explained how they shared the planet with cat-shifters called the Var who lived to the south of the Draig lands. He spoke of aliens landing occasionally and as that being their only real threat on the planet. Pointing to what she gathered was the west, he indicated they were starting an underground survey to possibly mine for ore to use in interplanetary trade—but that such a reality was still a long time away.

The light shifted from the greener tint to a bluer hue, in what she could assume indicated the evening hours. He didn't seem in a hurry to go back. Since she was enjoying the exploration she didn't protest when he brought them to a path in the forest and led her deeper in to the woods. Aside from the swooping of an occasional red bird of prey, they were alone.

"What do you think of your new kingdom, m'lady?"

"You have to stop saying things like that." Eve didn't want to feed this man's delusion, but eventually he would find out just what kind of person she was. "Some women are made to be queens. I'm not."

"But you accept this world very well. Can you not accept me?"

"There's something you need to understand about me, dragon man. I'm adaptable, so I can come to terms with a lot—even apparently being on an alien world. Not much surprises me and not much scares me. My parents were, let's just say they were not the reliable sort. They kicked me out of the family van when I was seventeen with a bag of ditch weed that I could either smoke or sell for cash, and they didn't look back. I sold it because I don't do drugs and needed food. My mother home-schooled me some when I was little, so I at least learned how to read. Sometimes they'd drop me off at a school, lie about transcripts being on the way, and used it like their own personal daycare. When people started asking too many questions, we'd take off."

He didn't speak. She'd shocked him? If so, it was for the best. Maybe then he could see why pursuing a relationship with her was a bad move.

"When food ran out, I stole from a farmer's market. I did send money when I had it, but I did steal and I knew it was wrong. I lived on the streets and did odd jobs so I could buy a guitar. I did a few street gigs and bought a better guitar. Being transient is the only thing I'm good at." She glanced back to where the village was beyond the trees. "I've been on my own a very long time. If this is where the wind has taken me for now, so be it. It's not like I have some white picket fence to run back to. I have an old tour van and random couches in the back of clubs. It's not glamorous, but I eat, I make music, I don't hurt anyone."

"Your parents abandoned you to starve?" He couldn't imagine. "And the people did not take you in and feed you?"

"I was seventeen. And what people? Foster care? They'd have kicked me out the moment I turned eighteen." She shrugged as if it didn't matter, but it did matter. It hurt deeply.

"I do not know what that is, but your people, other humans, should have made sure you never were hungry enough to steal. Here everyone contributes and everyone eats."

"Well, on my world not everyone contributes and not everyone eats."

He touched her arm and the contact sent tiny tremors over her. She wanted desperately to hold him against her, to kiss and touch, to lose herself in the pleasure his body promised. "I give you my word you will never starve."

"Can we talk about something else?" She shrugged off his hand and backed away. Eve didn't need him to fix her life or feel sorry for her. That's not why she told him.

"As you wish. How old are you now?" he asked. "The abandonment must have been a very long time ago."

Did he just call her super old?

"How old are you?" she shot back a little too quickly.

"I believe it translates roughly into sixty Earth years."

"Sixty?" Suddenly, she laughed, and he was glad for her smile. "I think you mean thirty."

"No, I am confident that it is at least sixty. Maybe seventy or more."

"Well, damn. Can I have the name of your surgeon?"

"Why?" He tried to reach for her. "Are you ill?" He glanced around the forest as if to look for help that he could send to fetch the doctor.

"It was a joke because you look so young for your age." Eve shook her head. "You really have to learn to relax, Kyran."

"You must be around my age," he said, "and you look young."

Eve snorted with laughter and grabbed her stomach. "I'm actually thirty. I see aging is different for our kind."

"Perhaps not. Here on our planet metabolism slows and people live longer." He reached to cup her cheek when she didn't meet his eyes. "The gods would not have paired us if we were not to live our full lives together."

"We're not married, Kyran. You just don't have a lot of experience with women here, so that's why you think that there is more between us. If you look at it logically, you will see that I am not queen material.

I've never lived in a real home. How can I adjust to a castle?"

"And you should look at us spiritually." Kyran reached for her hand. She hesitated before giving it to him. "I do not know if all this doubt is a human trait or simply yours, but you have to stop cycling things in your head and just feel the truth."

"But—"

He shook his head, cutting off her words. He took her hand and brought it beneath his shirt to rest over his heart. Her fingers trembled as she touched him. "Close your eyes, Eve, and know."

For some reason, she obeyed. Maybe she wanted his convictions to be true. No one had ever wanted her so terribly they were willing to cross portals for her. Kyran was kind and caring and patient. She felt that already. But now, as she touched him, she felt not only the warmth of his skin but a tingling thread being drawn from his heart into her. The sensation started as the prickling of pure emotion—heartache and fears, passion and pleasure, longing and pain, happiness and joy, rapture. The emotions collided in her like an offering of all life was and could be—not a sugarcoated fantasy but a reality that nothing was perfect but this could be close.

From the emotion of possibilities sprang forth a

stream of conscious thoughts. At first, it was merely words—*beautiful, heart, don't go, stay, stay...*

Eve gasped and opened her eyes as his voice sounded in her head. He had shifted and stood before her as a dragon. Intense eyes stared at her from the harder brown flesh his face had become.

"I can feel you are scared, not of me but of a rooted life," his voice said though his lips did not move.

"I," Eve whispered aloud. His head lowered slightly and she stopped talking. Instead, she tried to direct her thoughts back to him. *"I feel you begging me to...stay?"*

He smiled and nodded.

"You're worried if I go you won't ever find anyone else." Eve felt her shoulders slump some. *"But you're wrong, Kyran. You have so much to offer. I think you just don't understand Earth dating customs. I can help you. I—"*

"I feel you don't want to help me because you don't want me with anyone else. You love—"

Eve jerked her hand from his chest and stepped back to cut off the connection.

"It's too late," he continued to speak in her mind. *"The connection is formed. We are truly mated. Forever. I told you, this was blessed by the gods."*

Eve's gaze roamed down his body, automatically

looking over his shifted form. He had characteristics of what she'd call a medieval dragon, as if that creature mated with a man to create the Draig. Unable to deny the feelings swirling inside her, she stepped to him. Taking his face in her hands, she kissed him, not caring that he was unlike her. Hard skin melted into softer flesh and he kissed her back as a man.

"I told you, we cannot mate in shifted form," he whispered against her mouth.

"You're pretty confident you're going to get lucky." Eve grabbed him by his shirt and pulled him with her deeper into the forest as she looked for a place they could lie down.

"I am indeed very lucky, m'lady." He tugged her against his body and lifted her off the ground. She wrapped her arms around his neck. Her feet dangled as he walked.

"I said *get* lucky," she started to correct before she said, "Never mind. Yes, you're very lucky."

He smiled into their kiss before deepening it. Kyran laid her down slowly onto a bed of short fluffy plants. It felt like cotton against her skin. He skimmed his hand over her waist and lifted her shirt.

"You better not stop this time," Eve thought. Kyran chuckled, indicating he'd heard her.

The soft plants tickled her skin as he pulled her

shirt over her head. She wore her black bra. He fumbled with it, trying to pull it up like a shirt. Laughing, Eve pushed up to unhook it in the back.

Kyran removed his shirt and tossed it aside before leaning over her to kiss her stomach. He trailed his lips up the valley of her breasts. Eve's breath caught. Their bodies were connected by more than flesh. She felt as if his heart beat next to hers. When he breathed, she felt as if the air filled her lungs. His eyes flashed with gold, drawing her deeper under his spell.

With each aching sweep of his mouth, he stirred passion. Eve's toes curled and she arched up. Kyran unfastened the ties at her waist with deft fingers before tugging them off her legs. As she laid naked on the alien soil, she rubbed against the cottony bed.

Kyran stood and she watched him fully undress. The solid form of his muscles flexed beautifully. Dots of sunlight streamed through the trees to dance over his flesh. The hard length of his arousal stood powerfully tall from his hips, yet she felt no fear when his hips settled between her parted thighs.

Kyran splayed his fingers over her chest, gently holding her down. Mindless, she reached for him. He brought his free hand between her legs and intimately rubbed her sex. He slid in her moisture, circling the tight bud he found there.

Eve dug her heels into the ground and pressed her hips up. She moaned, begging him for more. Kyran let loose a low, rumbling primal sound in the back of his throat. Releasing her chest, he tugged her hips and angled his body for penetration. His cock brushed along her sex before he eased into her. Slowly, he filled her, stretching her so that her body could take him.

Eve gasped when he circled his hips, liking the way he hit her just right. It was as if he read her desires and knew just how to please her. A warm hand cupped her breast, delighting the hard nipple with tiny pinches. He thrust deeper, working in and out. The tension built. He rocked faster, harder. Eve stiffened, orgasming hard. Instantly, Kyran joined her, coming inside her.

Weakened in the aftermath of pleasure, she dropped her limbs to the ground and didn't move save to catch her breath.

Kyran kissed her lips and whispered, "I am a very lucky man."

CHAPTER ELEVEN

"IT IS DONE. WE HAVE JOINED," Kyran announced.

Shocked, Eve tried to stop walking but Kyran insistently led her into what appeared to be someone's private office. The king looked over from where he stood in front of a row of shelves that held rolled parchments. His hand dropped from where he'd been about to grab a scroll.

Eve's mouth opened but no sound came out. She was far from a prude, and granted, her childhood didn't exactly classify as normal, but she was pretty sure you didn't announce to your parents when you got laid. Regardless of what planet you lived on.

"Many blessings!" The king grinned. "The people will be happy to hear of this. You have set a fine example."

Eve tried to smile but knew her stunned expression couldn't have looked pleasant.

"If the rest of the princes find wives, this will solve our problems." King Severin approached Eve. "Well done, daughter. I can't believe I was worried that taking brides from Earth would end badly. You are a very agreeable species. Not at all contrary like the eldest of our elders have made humans out to be. Finding women should prove simple enough. We will have all the eligible males settled within a few years."

Eve didn't really feel like his words were a compliment. "Ah, exactly how many Earth women do you plan on kidnapping?"

"We are marrying them," Kyran corrected. "Giving them a home."

She felt his sincerity inside of her. The connection between them was strange, and she tried to block it. "Listen, just because I'm not freaking out on you more doesn't mean that all Earth women are like me. They expect to be wooed, romanced. Not just hit over the head and dragged through a portal to an alien land. Many of them will have boyfriends and families. You can't just get them drunk and lead them down the rabbit hole."

The king looked at his son and frowned.

Instantly, he darted forward and put Eve behind his back. "You *struck* your wife?"

"I would never," Kyran swore.

The king turned confused eyes to her. "Was it an accident? Why would you say my son struck you? No man shall ever strike his wife."

"My meaning was lost in translation." Eve made a mental note to be more literal. It would be hard. Sarcasm and sass didn't go away over night.

"So you have not been injured by my son?" the king insisted. "The joining was your doing?"

"He has been very kind." Eve inched back as the king stood extremely close. "And, uh..." She made a weak noise, sure she'd never been so mortified in all her life. "He did not hurt me when we, um, *joined*."

Slowly, the king nodded. "Good."

"Anyway, as I was trying to say, kidnapping women will not really go over well with the Earth government. It's also not fair to take women away from their homes without giving them a chance to decide for themselves. Things are very different since you left Earth. People are different." Eve glanced at Kyran. "And to tell you the truth, your guys looked a little comical—" The men gave her confused looks. "It was amusing. You sent a 1950s TV cowboy, a ninja, an outlaw biker and the sailor from—well, you wouldn't know the 70's music group I'm talking about."

"You make a good argument, m'lady," the king said. "You can instruct our men how to woo Earth women before they bring them home. You will start with Prince Finn and the Var princes."

Eve wasn't sure how he took her protest of kidnapping women to equal she was offering to set up a lonely shape-shifter intergalactic dating service. Then, seeing an opening, she nodded in agreement. "I'd be happy to help. But it would probably be best if I went with them through the portal."

To her utmost surprise, they both agreed in unison.

Just like that. Yes. She was free to travel back to Earth.

"See, the gods know," King Severin said to his son, grinning. "I will tell the queen of this arrangement. You should show the princess under the palace."

When they were alone, Kyran pulled her into his arms. "My father really just wants an excuse to seek out my mother."

"Under the palace?"

"The portal is in a cave system that runs under the palace. We actually created another entrance that requires less climbing and is reachable through the forest where we spent our first night together. However, it can still be reached by taking the stairwell down."

"So you will really let me go through the portal?" she asked. Somehow the idea of escaping didn't excite her as it should have. She should want to go home, but with Kyran's feelings swirling inside her, she was confused. Logic told her she needed to get away from him to think without his presence clouding her emotions.

"It is true not everyone is allowed to go through, but you, my princess, have very special knowledge that can benefit us greatly." Kyran swept her into his arms and held her as if it was the most natural thing in the world to hold his woman in such a way. Complete trust moved through them. She also felt his desire for her. It flowed openly as if he had no reason to hide anything from her.

"I know you wanted to dine with your family tonight, but do you think we might make other arrangements?" She tugged on his arm and gave him a meaningful look.

Kyran answered by carrying her through the door and rushing down the hall. Eve tossed back her head and laughed, lightly kicking her feet. One thing was certain. With Kyran, she would never be bored.

Kyran held his wife closer, wishing to never let her go. In all his years, he'd never understood just how life altering finding a mate really was. Eve was the piece he'd been missing without even realizing it.

His blood simmered at her nearness. The softness of her skin contrasted his harder muscles. How could he have known humans were so fragile? The delicateness of her called his protective instincts forth. She wasn't like the female dragons. Her eyes were playful and she said things that made no sense, and yet he always seemed to understand her.

"You are remarkable," he whispered, nestling his face into her hair. "I am truly blessed by the gods."

Eve made a small noise and placed her hand on the side of his face. "You're very lucky you did not pick up a high-strung woman, prince dragon." She started to laugh before stopping to add, "Hey, there's that guy again. I swear I see him everywhere."

Kyran turned only to catch a glimpse of a servant's tunic as the man turned a corner. He laughed. "He works in the palace. You will have to get used to seeing servants around."

Eve kicked her feet lightly. "Keep walking."

Kyran hurried with her through the halls toward their home. "I wish to be with you again."

She gave a sultry laugh. "Only if you promise me one thing."

"Anything your heart desires, m'lady."

"Don't go announcing to anyone afterward that we joined. I mean, sure people probably know we're having sex, but I'm not comfortable talking about it with your family."

It took a moment, but he realized what she meant. "You think...no, no. I said our joining was done, our connection as mates. It is the final step to marriage."

Eve blushed. "Oh, okay, good, so he wasn't talking about me sleeping with you."

Kyran shook his head in denial and felt her relief. "Not at all."

Once inside their home, he carried her to the bedroom. She practically melted against him, her body relaxing into his. Eve pressed kisses to his neck, each touch sending a shiver along his body.

He laid her on the bed and eagerly stripped out of his clothing. Eve pushed her pants from her hips, baring her legs. Kyran paused mid-movement to stare at her. Emotion overwhelmed him and he couldn't speak. This was everything a man could want—a wife, hope of a family, a future he could commit to.

Eve grinned and took off her shirt. She threw it at him. "Come here already."

Kyran obeyed, crawling over her. Her lips parted, accepting his kiss. She lifted her arms and spread her legs, accepting his body. She made tiny noises of pleasure, so soft and feminine. He never wanted to stop kissing her.

He ran his hand over her naked hip. The contact of their skin caused an electrical current to run between them. He felt her desire as if it were his own. Eve closed her eyes, gasping and trembling.

They made love slowly, exploring and discovering. When he finally entered her, pressing his arousal into her warmth, the moment was perfection. Only when he felt her body tremble did he let himself have release.

"My princess," he whispered against her neck.

She wound her fingers into his hair. "Meeting you has been a surreal adventure."

CHAPTER TWELVE

KYRAN FELT his wife wasn't in the room the moment he opened his eyes. Stretching his arms, he tossed the covers aside and hopped off the platform bed. Excitement filled him at the thought of Eve. He wanted to shift and run the forest, roaring his happiness to the trees. He wanted to hold her forever, worship at her feet, make love to her until they couldn't move. He didn't need his head to tell him what his heart innately knew. She was made for him. He'd known it the first moment he saw her on stage. Her song had been a shockwave that shook him to his very core.

"I love you, Eve," he whispered, never having been so sure of anything in his life.

Eager to tell her, he found himself tossing on

clothes and going in search of her. She wasn't in their home. The connection they shared was still new, but he tried to sense her location anyway. He detected nothing. Letting the shift ripple over his body, he closed his eyes and breathed deeply to catch her scent. It was faint but there.

Without thought, he followed her trail. To his surprise, it led him deeper into the palace, away from the main section to the narrow old tunnels and finally the steep stairwell. His heart pounded heavily. He'd told Eve about the tunnels. It had never occurred to him that she would use them to leave him.

The old tunnels were treacherous, which was why the shifters never used them, but he smelled her down there amongst the damp stone. In fact, it was the only thing his dragon senses could focus on— finding his wife.

He heard the activated portal before he saw the soft purple glow of its power. The valley entrance was blocked and so the air of the cave was stagnant. Dragons and cats were carved into the stone chamber, pointing away from the portal, a symbol of their exodus from Earth.

The elders called it magic. Their scholars called it technology. Kyran didn't know who to believe, he only knew that the portal worked. Without thought, he went after his wife. He couldn't force her to stay with him, but he wouldn't let her go without a fight. He would tell her how he felt. He would beg her to stay, for without her, he could never be whole.

CHAPTER THIRTEEN

PASSING through the portal stirred Eve's memories. However, she didn't have time to dwell on them as she was tossed to the hard ground on the other side. Her body tingled from the trip, the pins and needles of slowed blood returning to normal speed. She felt as if a piece of herself had been ripped out, left behind with her dragon-shifter husband.

Husband. The very thought caused her to fill with joy and sorrow. It was the first time she'd allowed herself to think of him in such a way. But something had happened in her short time with him. She'd found her purpose. She'd found a family. The full ache of having that ripped from her left sharp pain in her chest. It was true when people said you didn't know fully what you had until it was taken away. Desperation filled her and she tried to crawl back to the portal—only it was gone. She was trapped on Earth.

"Get up," a gruff voice demanded.

Eve looked up at the shifted cat-man who stood over her. Kyran had called him a servant, but she wasn't as sure. When he'd first approached her, she'd ignored her instinct to run. Oh, why hadn't she run? Years on the street had taught her to trust her gut. This man had been following her. She shouldn't have ignored it.

She looked behind her to the cracked rock wall that they'd come through for a hint of how to get back to Kyran. It was useless. The portal was gone. How would Kyran find her? Would he even know to look? When she left him he'd been sleeping. Not wanting to wake him with her insomnia, she'd merely thought to walk the halls. They were peaceful and quiet in the night hours.

"Just tell me what you want?" Eve said, not for the first time.

"I want your kind off my planet. Your weak blood will taint ours, turn us feeble." Brown hair framed wild eyes as he reached for her. At least he'd shifted back into his man form. He grabbed her arm and dragged her toward an old white building she didn't recognize. Shouts sounded in the distance followed by singing. They emerged from their hidden alcove to a courtyard. His eyes glowed with the power of his shift, but there was more. There was hate in his gaze, disgust. He sniffed the air and curled his lips. "Such drunken filth. Your kind has no discipline."

Eve's heart pounded as they made their way through the dark yard. As they pushed through an iron door into a narrow street, she saw a sign that read *Old Ursuline Convent, Louisiana.*

"We're in New Orleans?" The question was more a confirmation of her surprise than an actual question. He quickened his pace, forcing her to move. "I thought the portal went to Ohio."

"It goes to a different place each Earth night, so do not think of ever finding it again." He gripped her arm tighter as a group of people crossed the street. She felt his claws digging into her flesh. Eve had seen this man shift when she tried to run from him and knew that the drunken college kids taking a haunted history tour would be no match for a cat-shifter. "Not that I have to worry about you after tonight."

"What do you mean?" Eve demanded.

"This is the Lalaurie Mansion, recognized not only as one of the most haunted houses in the French Quarter, but perhaps in all of the United States," the tour guide boasted. "It is now owned by a very famous celebrity, but he never stays here—not since he heard the stories I'm about to tell you about its previous owner, Madame Delphine Lalaurie."

The cat-shifter stopped and glanced up the three-story mansion on the corner of the block, as if considering taking her inside the empty home.

"You got me back to Earth," Eve said. "Now just go."

She was sure she could find her way back to the place they'd come through the portal. If she found that, she'd find a way to get back to Qurilixen, to Kyran, to the man she wanted to spend forever with.

"Ghosts aren't real," a man heckled the crowd, sounding more angry than mischievous. "Get out of the way. Sidewalks are for pedestrians. You know, pedestrians, it's from the Latin for to walk, not for to stand."

"You're a dumbass," someone answered him. "Sober up!"

The cat-shifter aggressively led her around the corner, away from the group into an empty street. They kept moving away from the crowd.

"Just go," Eve said. "I'm off your planet. Mission accomplished. No need to hurt anyone here."

"I saw you in the woods," he stated.

"What?"

"I followed you. I saw you join with him. Even now you might carry his child. I cannot allow a shifter to be born in your world. I cannot risk your people trying to find us. The portal should never have been reopened, and after I'm finished, it will never be again."

"I thought you needed women." Eve tried desperately to keep him talking. She saw the deadly intent in his eyes.

"Shifter women," he clarified. "It's only a matter of time before we are blessed once more. We cannot lose faith by allowing humans into our world. Any child you bear will be an aberration."

The man continued to mumble under his breath, but she could not understand the Qurilixian language. She felt the bite of his claws in her arm and the wet trickle of blood as he punctured the skin.

Eve ignored the pain. "If we're so awful, why come here at all? Why not kill me back home? Scared the others will find out what you did, coward?"

"And let your human filth rot on our sacred planet?" The very idea seemed to make him shudder in revulsion.

A man came striding around the corner wearing absolutely nothing but a short pink tutu. She never thought she'd be so glad to see a crazy eccentric so much in her life. Mr. Tutu marched with purpose, and the sight of his pale naked ass was enough to distract her captor long enough for her to rip her arm free. Eve didn't hesitate. She ran back the way they'd come.

The cat-shifter gave chase. He growled. The noise caused her to run faster. She turned the corner in front of Lalaurie Mansion. The tour had moved along, their absence emptying the street to being nearly abandoned.

Another growl sounded as she was hit in the back. Eve flew forward and braced herself for a hard concrete landing. Instead, arms caught her and she instantly knew she was safe.

"Kyran," she said in surprise even before she looked up to confirm what her body knew.

"Are you injured?" he demanded. Eve shook her head in denial and he pushed her behind his back.

The second she was shoved to safety, he shifted and charged forward. Her husband's roar met with the cat's growl. Talons formed on Kyran's outstretched hand as his body hardened with brown armor. The cat-shifter leapt. Blond fur sprouted on his features and covered his forearms. He didn't fully turn into a feline, but to a standing cat.

Eve had seen Kyran shift, but the full extent of what that meant became incredibly clear. The cat slashed. Kyran deflected the blow and swung the man up and over so that he was launched into the air.

"Yeah!" someone yelled. The noise soon attracted others and a crowd began to gather. The cat slammed into the street, only to instantly push back to his feet to keep fighting.

"Get him!" another screamed.

"Whoo-hoo!"

"Yeah!"

Eve ignored the onlookers. She tried to find an opening to help Kyran. Though it was evident he didn't need her help. He held his own.

The shifters fought their way down the street, toward the convent. The crowds followed, cheering and clapping. Eve screamed as Kyran was slammed into the wall. She surged forward to thump her fists against the cat-shifter's back. Before she made contact, Kyran kicked, launching the man over the wall into the convent yard. Kyran leapt high into the air as he propelled himself over the wall to give chase.

The crowd clapped wildly now that the show was over. Eve looked for a way to go after the shifters. She felt people pressing forward. She turned, lifting her hands to push them back. Only they shoved money at her, tipping her for the performance.

Eve tried to smile, well aware that Kyran would want her to keep the dragon-shifter secret even though he'd just battled down the French Quarter. When finally she broke free of the crowd, she ran down the sidewalk to the iron gate they'd used to leave the convent's courtyard. Once inside, she found Kyran coming back from the portal alone.

"What happened?" She ran for him.

"He's dead," Kyran said. "I pushed him through to our side so he would not be found by humans."

"How? The portal closed." Eve wrapped her arms around his neck.

"No, it's only hidden. If you touch the wall it will pull you in. Once activated, the portal will remain open for several hours."

Holding him tight, she whispered, "I was so scared I'd never see you again."

"I should have listened when you said you felt like we were being followed. I'm sorry I didn't see it. The Var have never attacked us."

"He said he didn't want human blood polluting the shifter gene pool." Eve began to shake violently now that it was over. Tears streamed down her face.

"He was going to kill me. He...he...you came. I didn't know if you would find me."

"I will always come for you, my princess. You are as much of me as my own heart." Kyran held her tighter. "I was worried you'd left me to come back here."

Eve opened herself up to him, letting him feel her emotions—relief, happiness, love. "I love you, Kyran. I should have said it sooner."

He smiled and nodded. "I feel it. I love you, m'lady. But when you were gone I worried you'd decided a life with me wouldn't be enough. I saw you on stage with your music."

"Yes, I do want to visit Earth, and I will, with you. As for music, I can make music anywhere. All I need is a guitar and my voice. And who knows, maybe I'll find some dragons and start a band." She stroked her fist against his cheek.

He pulled at her wrist so he could look at her hand. "What is this?"

"Oh," Eve had forgotten she clutched the money. "Locals thought you were street performers putting on a show. They tipped you."

"For fighting?"

She nodded. "If you're going to go full-out dragon in the middle of a city, you picked the right one. New Orleans embraces the strange and unusual. You blended right in."

"The gods truly bless us," he said. "Shall we go home?"

Eve looked at her closed fists and then toward the hidden alcove where the portal was. "Not quite yet. We need to go on a small errand first."

"You wish to use the trading paper to get a guitar?"

Eve laughed. "It's going to take more than one fight to earn enough for a guitar."

"Then?"

"Cheeseburgers," she stated, keeping the money in her fist as she wrapped an arm around his waist. "We're going to buy lots and lots of cheeseburgers. You can buy me a guitar later."

"Mm," he moaned thoughtfully. "I should like to see your cheeseburger ritual. I did not realize we are near the water so that you may enjoy it in your hip coverings."

"You think cheeseburgers are only for the beach?"

He nodded eagerly. "I have seen your transmissions." Kyran opened his mouth and gave a slow lick of his lips, mimicking a very seductive fast food commercial model.

A jolt of desire filled her at the gesture and she quickened her pace. "Well done, dragon. That's exactly how you eat it." They slipped through the gate to the street. "By the way, I won your little game. I never said I am your wife and you are my prince before having sex with you."

"Aw, but you did tell me, wife," Kyran pointed at her chest and then rested his hand over his heart. "And I heard it clearly, here."

"I can't argue with that." She accepted his kiss, stopping to press her body against his. His arousal formed against her stomach. "Mm, we'd better make those cheeseburgers to go."

"Always as you wish, my bride."

The End

THE SERIES CONTINUES...

REBELLIOUS PRINCE

Captured by a Dragon-Shifter Book Two

Cat-shifter Prince Rafe knows that technically he's supposed to be going to Earth to find a bride, but he doesn't see the need to rush things. While his dragon-shifter neighbors appear all too eager to claim their mates and settle down, he's all for putting that final moment off and enjoying his little trips through the portal. Yeah, yeah, eventually he'll have to marry and set a good example for his people because on his planet females are rare and they need to have children and blah blah blah. But honestly, cat-shifters are known to embrace their feral side and it would take a very impressive female to tame his.

Then he sees Jenna Kearney and all bets are off.

Chapter One Excerpt

Kansas City, Kansas

"Hello, *faes*, want to take a ride on my spaceship?" Rafe shot the Earth women a playful smile and wagged his brows. They giggled just as he knew they would. Even on his home planet of Qurilixen he had a way with the ladies—well, what very few single ladies were left on his planet, and the alien travelers who visited. What could he say? Charm was a gift. Half the time it didn't even matter what he said to them, as long as he dipped his voice and smiled.

"I don't care if he is crazy, look at him," one of the women whispered. She had no way of knowing his shifter hearing could pick up her hushed words.

Rafe was technically supposed to be looking for a bride while on Earth being as humans were reproductively compatible. It was the whole reason the shifter princes were allowed to leave their home world. Rafe was part of the cat-shifting Var royal family who ruled half the planet—the fun half. The other half was ruled by the dragon-shifting Draig. As much as he liked his dragon neighbors, they were a little reserved and obsessed with planning the future.

Since the portal to Earth was on their land, they were only willing to open it if the princes looked for life mates.

All the dragons ever talked about was mating and continuing the family lines...kind of like Rafe's older brother, Prince Ivar. For a cat, Ivar seemed to be missing the wild gene.

Rafe grinned. He was wild enough for both of them. His trips to Earth were solely for adventure. The culture captivated him. The plentiful sea of women fascinated him, especially since his planet lacked that particular resource—females. Men they had plenty of.

He didn't stop to talk to the flirtatious women as he went to the diner's counter. If he forgot to acquire cheeseburgers for the Draig princess, he'd never hear the end of it. Princess Eve was the first and only human to be brought through the portal and the only demand she ever made was for Earth food. She'd married dragon-shifter Prince Kyran. The union was a good one. It proved portal travel for brides worked and allowed the three remaining Qurilixian princes to continue their explorations offworld.

Rafe knew why their parents wanted them to mate so badly. Scholars estimated that the shifters would die out within a generation if women weren't brought to the planet. No matter how many babies a woman had, the vast majority came out male. Scientists tried, but no one could explain it. People were healthy, lived longer lives—much longer than they had on Earth—and for the most part thrived. They just didn't conceive girl babies.

The downside of Kyran finding love after one attempt through the portal was that their royal parents were starting to get a little suspicious when no one else brought back a bride. Rafe liked Princess Eve well enough. She was what the Earth people called a spitfire. And, thanks to her help, he and his fellow shifters were able to blend successfully in to the modern human world. None of this meant Rafe was ready to find his own princess.

Since shifters had originated on Earth centuries ago, they still spoke a dialect of one of the Earth languages, but so much had changed since they'd left, and many things had to be learned. What little the elders remembered about escaping to Qurilixen was outdated and filled with stories of shifter persecution and bloody war. For this reason, they hid their shifting abilities while traveling. Not counting a couple bar brawls when Rafe had tried to seduce a claimed woman—not that he could detect a mark or

finger shackle on her to back up the man's claim—
Rafe hadn't seen much by the way of Earth battle.

Night pushed its way past the broken streetlight
to darken the diner windows. The waitress behind
the counter came forward with her notepad to take
his order. He leaned forward on his hands. "I'm
wondering if you have a smile for me, sweetheart."

Startled, the woman blinked rapidly and then
started to laugh. She swiped her pen at him before
saying, "What can I get for you?"

"A dozen cheeseburgers and do you have something called cream pie?"

"Chocolate, banana, coconut—"

"A slice of each. To leave." Rafe turned as the
bell on the door dinged to signify someone entered.

"I think you mean to go," the waitress said.

Rafe absently nodded as he studied the new
woman who entered. His accent made it easier to
cover his English mistakes. He was about to answer
when the woman pushed a hood off her head. Red
hair spilled over her shoulders. The sides were
clipped back to reveal small ears. A strong force hit
him and he couldn't move.

"Evening Jenna," the waitress called.

"Hi Barb," the redhead answered. She turned,

pretty green eyes looking past him to the waitress. "Usual please."

"Hey, spaceman," one of the women he'd flirted with earlier called. "Come sit with us."

"Joe's already started it for you, hon," Barb answered Jenna. "Be up in a minute."

"Thanks. I didn't have a chance to eat today." Jenna crossed the diner, pulling the strap of her messenger bag off her chest and over her head before shrugging out of her jacket.

"You mean you forgot to eat today. Again." Barb poured a coffee next to him and slid it toward the woman. "Sit down before you pass out."

Jenna came toward the counter. Rafe inhaled, detecting the scent of flowers in her hair. He stared at her. The sound of her voice mesmerized him. Jenna reached for the coffee and finally glanced up. He held his breath to hear what she would say to him.

Jenna arched a brow. "Your alien groupies are waiting for you, spaceman."

Rafe let loose his breath. "You know I am not from Earth?"

The woman stiffened, eyeing him as if he suddenly resembled the back end of a yorkin beast. She brushed past him and took a booth as far from the counter as she could get. Setting her bag on the

156

table, she began rifling through papers and did not look at him again.

Rafe ignored the noisy women and they soon lost interest in his joining them. He sat at the counter to wait for his order and watched the redhead. She didn't look up, and he couldn't look away.

Jenna did not look like the Earth women he normally met. In clubs he could see at least sixty percent of a woman's body. Jenna appeared more reserved. Loose slacks and a blue striped button down shirt covered very lush curves. This woman hadn't reacted to his charming smile either. He found himself intrigued.

"Burgers be up soon. Here's the pie." Barb put a bag on the counter in front of him. "You're barking up the wrong tree there, lover boy."

"I do not bark," Rafe said.

"Whatever you say." Barb left.

Rafe lifted the bag of pie slices and made his move toward the table. At his presence, she mumbled, "Thanks. Just leave it on the table."

"You wish to eat my cream?" Rafe asked.

The woman gave a little jump of surprise and looked up at him. Her mouth opened but no sound came out as she looked from his face to his hips and back up again.

"I have very good cream," Rafe said, hoping to see her smile at him. "I would enjoy it if you ate—"

"I-I..." Jenna held up her hand. "Are you... unwell? I mean, do you need...mental help?"

Rafe didn't understand her question. He smiled at her, waiting for the dip of her eyes and the tiny giggle females on this planet made. She had such a pretty voice and an even prettier face. "I am Rafe and I do not require assistance at this moment."

Rafe slid into the booth across from her and reached into his bag to lift a white container. "I have chocolate, banana—"

"Oh, pie, you have cream pie," Jenna said, seeming to relax. "No. I don't eat pie."

"Ah, you eat parchment," he pushed at the pages on the table. They were filled with numbers and charts. Finally, she gave a small smile. The look caused his heart to quicken and his stomach to tighten.

"I don't know what your game is, sitting down here, talking to me." Jenna gathered her papers and shoved them into her bag.

He glanced out the window, knowing he had to go just as soon as he had Princess Eve's food. Eve liked burgers to the point she threatened him if he came home empty-handed—well, not a real threat, but an almost real threat. "I have cheeseburgers. Would you like to eat that?"

"Do you have a food fetish? Is that what this is?" She shook her head. "I'm honestly not in the mood. I'm behind on paperwork for a thankless boss who is threatening layoffs because of the economy. The hot water in my shower is broken and my landlord is a deadbeat. And I lost my cat to old age. So, please, I don't need crazy right now. Just go be an alien with your girlfriends over there."

Rafe glanced over his shoulder. "Those girls are not my friends. You said you had not eaten today." Then seeing Barb placing his bag on the counter, he knew he didn't have much time. He hesitated. Something about Jenna made him want to stay.

"Barb, can I take mine to go, please?" Jenna asked loudly.

"Sure thing, hon." Barb disappeared into the back.

"Looks like your order is ready. You should pick it up now." Jenna gave a pointed look at the counter.

Rafe slowly stood and nodded. "As you so decree, m'lady."

Updated Reading List and Links here:
MichellePillow.com

ABOUT MICHELLE M. PILLOW

New York Times & *USA TODAY*
Bestselling Author

Michelle loves to travel and try new things, whether it's a paranormal investigation of an old Vaudeville Theatre or climbing Mayan temples in Belize. She believes life is an adventure fueled by copious amounts of coffee.

Newly relocated to the American South, Michelle is involved in various film and documentary projects with her talented director husband. She is mom to a fantastic artist. And she's managed by a dog and cat who make sure she's meeting her deadlines.

For the most part she can be found wearing pajama pants and working in her office. There may or may not be dancing. It's all part of the creative process.

Come say hello! Michelle loves talking with readers on social media!

www.MichellePillow.com

facebook.com/AuthorMichellePillow

twitter.com/michellepillow

instagram.com/michellempillow

bookbub.com/authors/michelle-m-pillow

goodreads.com/Michelle_Pillow

amazon.com/author/michellepillow

youtube.com/michellepillow

pinterest.com/michellepillow

COMPLIMENTARY EXCERPTS

TAKING KARRE

BY MICHELLE M. PILLOW

Divinity Warriors Book Four
Alternate Reality Romance

Sir Vidar of Spearhead is too busy guarding the borderlands to bother with the headache of selecting a bride. Ordered to marry by the king, he plans to grab a woman and get back to the warfront, never to think of it again. That is until he meets the alluring Lady Karre with her teasing eyes, lush lips and irresistible ways.

Known by many names, inter-dimensional thief Karre, has only one purpose—take down the company that ruined her life. When her luck runs out and she's caught, Divinity Corporation condemns her to matrimony on a primitive, warrior-filled plane where Karre soon discovers there are worse fates than being prisoner to a man with insatiable appetites.

Before long, days and nights filled with bliss becomes something neither expected, and when Karre is taken, Vidar is forced to confront emotions a battle-hardened warrior never expected to feel.

Taking Karre Prologue Excerpt

Three weeks ago, Dimensional Plane 395, Adult Pleasure Centre VWH
Because right now, in this moment, she was their fantasy.

Karre marched out on stage in red stiletto heels, a slinky dress, big grin and nothing else. She kept tempo with the hard, drumming beat of music. Men hollered, whooping their excitement just to see her. She smiled at them, looking over the crowd of heads. She could make them do anything—beg, buy, steal, kill—because right now, in this moment, she was their fantasy.

Blonde hair piled high on her head, garnished

with a string of diamonds and rubies some suitor had given her. It was a sweet trinket, one she might even keep, not that she would remember where the jewels came from. She traveled too much and had more important things on her mind.

Karre turned slowly with her arms raised above her head. The hem of her short dress lifted to just below the curve of her ass. When her back was to the crowd, she bent forward. The cheering grew as the men got a peek of the naked treasure hidden beneath the clinging silver. What did she care if they saw her ass? Her pussy? Her breasts? They were just skin, flesh, a tool like any other. No matter how much they wanted her, they would never be able to touch her.

On this dimensional plane of existence, humans cohabitated with humanoid creatures. The first time Karre saw a vampire sucking on the neck of a shifted werewolf, she'd nearly sprinted out of the room to find her wrist portal to flash out of there to another plane. The portable device looked like a large bracelet to most, but to Karre it was her sole means of survival.

Necessity made her stay where she was. This plane was the easiest to get jewels on without resorting to thievery and the hard, shiny rocks were good for trade in nearly every dimension. Besides, not counting the dancing, being in Dimensional Plane 395 was like taking a vacation. With so many strange and different creatures, they never questioned anything she said and most were focused more on blood-drinking and pleasure-seeking.

Being in a new dimensional plane was like being in your world, but only if had it evolved in a different way. To a point, there were many similarities. Languages, generally, were relatively similar, though for some reason the written word consisted of unfamiliar symbols. Some people looked the same, but were not the same people. Natural disasters and major human events were shared. Weather was the same and each place was still Earth.

"I adore you, Sparkle!" a man yelled. "Marry me!"

Karre turned to look over her shoulder at the crowd and winked. A plethora of large green horns, red flesh, reptile skin, webbed fingers, sharp fangs, and ridged flesh stretched out before her until the mass became a single entity flowing back and forth like a wave.

"I'll take that as a yes," the same voice answered her playful flirting. A rush of similar proposals followed the first, showering her in declarations of love. But she wasn't fool enough to believe them. What they felt wasn't love. It was lust.

Karre knew their adoration for what it was and used it to fuel her dance. She twirled and wiggled, thrust her ass toward them, drew her hips in seductive circles, only to pause in a sexy pose in time with the music. Slowly, she undressed, peeling the slinky gown off her body. Several lights flashed, illuminating her from various angles, leaving no curve unseen.

Just flesh. Just a means. Just another job. Just another plane and soon a distant memory.

Her smile widened, as she knew this was her last dance, at least for this trip. The cheering rose, but she stopped listening. And then it was over. Karre held still, letting the dying notes find their silence before walking naked from the stage.

"You were wonderful tonight, Sparkle," a new dancer fawned. "The crowd loves you. I was wondering if you'd show me how to—"

"Is he here?" Karre asked, stopping the woman from starting a conversation Karre didn't have time for. It's not like she could tell the truth—that all her dancing skill was someone else's memories uploaded into her brain by a device she'd bartered for on another plane.

"He's in your room," the woman answered, frowning slightly at having her question dismissed. "And he brought a large case. I think it's full of gifts so you'll consider his suit."

"Perfect," Karre grinned. Taking a long robe the woman held out, she slipped it over her shoulders. "I don't want to be disturbed."

Two weeks ago, Dimensional Plane 154, Stac Lesh Mansion
Because right now, in this moment, she was the help.

Karre stared at her red, curly hair in the liquid-silver reflection wall. It had been pulled into a bun at the nape of her neck. The long skirt of the plain uniform and padded body suit did much to hide her figure under the thick gray wool. An apron, changed every time so much as a spot marred the pristine white, covered high over her chest and low to her knees. With the clothes and makeup to pale her face into an unimpressive mask, no one would look twice in her direction because right now, in this moment, she was the help.

She had expected to keep her head down and do her job for months before coming back into this room. But in putting on the uniform, she became invisible. The rich people she worked for didn't look in her direction twice. Well, that wasn't necessarily true. When the wife was gone, the husband had looked at her more than twice. A big grin showcasing blacked-out teeth and a very inappropriately timed belch had changed his interest quickly.

Karre reached to touch her reflection. Behind her, the rich baby's room spread out like the entrance to a palace. Gilded ceilings etched with clouds, golden rays of light and ridiculously cheerful fat angels stretched above as white marble stretched below. It was cold and unwelcoming and more than any one person deserved.

"Oh, wonderful, finally, help," the rich wife said, sweeping into the room. Karre didn't bother to learn the lady's name. "Rich wife" was much easier to remember. The woman held her child under the arms, away from her chest, as if contact with the baby would somehow ruin her carefully planned outfit. "Which one are you?"

"Brigitte, ma'am."

"Take Cinny," the woman ordered. "Mommy needs time to collect herself."

Karre suppressed her groan of frustration at being interrupted and stood to dutifully take the child. She cradled the poor creature close and walked it toward the crib.

"Sing to Cinny before you put her down," rich wife ordered, standing before the liquid silver as she brushed at her clothes.

Karre stopped walking. Sing? To the gurgling, wiggling mass in her arms?

"Well, Brigitte?"

"Mistress, mistress, let me come in," Karre sang the only childlike-sounding song she could think of at the moment, pausing to clear her throat. "I have the pence if you have a quim."

"What a pretty tune," the woman said. "I've never heard it. What does it mean?"

"My dad sang it to my mom," Karre answered, letting the memories she had uploaded into her mind take over her personality—Brigitte of the Fallen Women, a whore's daughter raised in a brothel, adept at blending into new environments. She left off the word "once" before adding the lie, "I'm not sure what it means."

"Carry on."

"Mistress, mistress, I'm stiff as a pin. I need your..." Karre continued, lowering her voice as the woman left her alone with the gurgling, oblivious child. Stopping, she laid the baby down and said, "Sorry, kid, it's the only song I knew the words to. But I guess it's all right. I turned out just fine with lots of jewels and pretty things and you're too little to understand what any of it means. You should be more worried about growing up in this place with that mom of yours. Now, if you just be good," she paused and tucked a blanket around the infant's body, "I've got a job to do."

Going back to the wall, Karre again reached for her reflection. She stepped forward, letting the liquid hit her hand. It stung, freezing cold in the warm room. For a moment, she hesitated, glancing back at the gurgling child. She thought about grabbing Cinny and taking the baby with her.

"Sorry, kid," she whispered, "even with that mother, you're better off here."

It was a delicate balance—keeping her purpose in her mind while living out the personality and quirks of another—almost like having two people in her head. Karre's hand met with the wall as she felt around, searching for the device she'd hidden. When her fingers met with a smooth, flat surface, she frowned. Putting a second hand to the wall she became frantic, sliding her palms in wide, searching arcs. Perhaps the adhesive she used had come loose. She bent her knees, crouching as she searched the bottom corner of the liquid reflecting wall. Her fingers were so cold it became hard to feel, but the molecular structure of the liquid kept the silver from trickling down her arms as it remained bonded to itself.

Then, to her great surprise, warmth gripped her. A hand wrapped her wrist and jerked her forward. She was pulled through the wall, feeling the sting of silver before landing on a hard, stone floor. Gasping and shivering, she looked around the secret room. A wall of computing towers lined one side, next to three technicians silently typing away on their holographic keypads.

"Lose something, Brigitte?" a man asked, coming close.

Karre glanced up from the floor, "No, sir. I have nothing to lose."

"You are extraordinary." The man laughed. Her eyes instantly took in the familiar insignia of the Divinity Corporation. "Finally, we meet."

Karre forced a grin she didn't feel, letting him see her blackened teeth. Knowing what she looked like, she couldn't help but wonder at his choice of words.

Extraordinary? "I wasn't aware we were destined to meet, sir. How lucky for me."

"I can assure you when I'm done with you, you won't feel lucky." The man leaned down, studying her face. He had the militant rigidity of a soldier, from the purposeful jerks of his body to the engraved frown lines around his mouth and eyes. His hard gaze bored into her, filling her with cold dread. She, or rather Brigitte, had seen that look in men's eyes before. They were usually the kind to beat a prostitute the second they couldn't get their pricks hard.

"I've heard that one before," she mumbled, pretending to be unimpressed.

"I'm Director Tomes and..." He paused, lifting the small, wrist-wrapping device she'd been searching the liquid-silver wall for. Divinity had the only known source of top-secret inter-dimensional travel technology and they wouldn't like the fact that someone had stolen it. "I have a feeling you know where I am from. It was very naughty of you to borrow our only portable jump prototype. Our scientists will be very interested in seeing how you got it to work. This device will make traveling to uncharted worlds much easier. No more carting around temporary portals. No more perfectly timed pickups from headquarters. No more rescue parties."

Less supervision so you can do more dark deeds, Karre silently added.

"We'll be able to explore planes at a much faster rate," Tomes continued, as if it was a good thing.

Just like an infectious disease.

"Sorry, I'm not available for science lessons, but if you'd like to make an appointment, I'm sure I can fit you in," Karre hummed in pretend thought, "uh, never."

"Oh, you're going to be fun to break, my dear," Tomes promised. "Talbert. Get her ready to go."

For a complete, up-to-date booklist, visit www. MichellePillow.com

PLEASE LEAVE A REVIEW

THANK YOU FOR READING!

Please take a moment to share your thoughts by leaving a review.

Be sure to check out Michelle's other titles at

www.michellepillow.com